THE KII

JOSEPH D LACEY

Stonegarden.net Publishing
http://www.stonegarden.net

Reading from a different angle.
California, USA

ISBN: 1-60076-141-0

StoneGarden.net Publishing
3851 Cottonwood Dr.
Danville, CA 94506

First StoneGarden.net Publishing paperback printing:
August 2009

Visit StoneGarden.net Publishing on the web at
http://www.stonegarden.net.

Cover art and design by James Grant

Chapter One

Night falls like a hammer-blow because we dread it. What you wish for is delayed, what you fear is swiftly delivered.

It begins with the sound of people crying. Hundreds, maybe more. They've lost something treasured and they want it back. Now the first gunshots; a few singles, the sound of booted feet running on cold sidewalks and empty streets. Then volleys of gunfire, coordinated and precise. More running, faint shouts of caution or command. Nearby the shots sound like firecrackers, farther away they're just popguns, hardly real. We all listen to the night sounds because it would be wrong, disrespectful somehow, to ignore them. Each of us waits for screams and prays we never hear them.

If I try really hard, I can remember the true sound of the city at night. Cars and sirens and a million tyres breathing over tar-bound stones. Jets and choppers sparkling and slicing up the air above us. People yelling, music passing by.

All we retain now are the gunshots. Once they were the sound of anger snapping and of private wars. Now, against the silence of the city, they are the sounds of survival.

"Crewing tonight, Sheri?" asks Ike.

"No. You?"

"What do you think?"

Ike Delgado never crews if he can help it. Doesn't have the belly for it. He's only asking so he knows if he's getting laid or not. Now he thinks he is.

He isn't.

"I'm doing spam and beans Delgado accompanied by a '98 Beaujolais. Want to join me?"

"I've got my period."

Ike hates blood. Especially from what he calls the axe-wound. He tries to hide his squirming and does a pretty good job.

"Doesn't mean we can't have dinner together."

"It does if I'm not hungry."

He shrugs, smiles. Somehow it's not nasty.

"More for me."

My turn to shrug. Then he says:

"Want to sleep at my place tonight?"

And suddenly we're in new territory. I don't like the look of it.

"Maybe tomorrow, Ike."

He shrugs again, then leaves.

Now I'm alone, sitting on an upturned soda crate in Sally Alley cleaning and oiling my guns. My period is actually a couple of days late. Been irregular ever since the Long Silence began. I'm crabby as hell because I haven't crewed for almost a week. The gun barrels are pleading for heat. Or maybe it's PMS.

Either way, Ike Delgado sleeps alone tonight. Sheri Foley needs space.

It doesn't take much discipline but it takes guts. If there'd been any soldiers who'd survived, maybe they could have taught us more about maintaining order amidst the chaos. Keeping our boots shiny and guns lubed while the body count rises. Marching and singing to keep our spirits up. But no soldiers made it or, if they did, they don't live in the Station. It doesn't matter. We've learned how to do the necessary. It's probably not quite enough knowledge to stay alive.

The crew goes out every night. It's a lottery. Anyone can volunteer but only seven take the shift. If something goes wrong, we only lose a few. We keep tally of the numbers – how many of them we dust, how many of us are left.

What we got:

A city block of shops, apartments and alleyways. Two gun stores. Three mini markets, two restaurants and a wholesale warehouse. One pharmacy. A few years supply of LPG in portable tanks. Rainwater catchments on every roof. Some grow bags and a few seeds. A wall at the end of each alley made of demolition leftovers and other salvage. More living space than we can use. About two hundred souls. I don't know how many we started out with but we're counting down to zero as the months go by.

What they got:

Uncountable numbers. Unpredictable requirements. Insomnia.

I just want to put you in the picture. There's more to it – a lot more – but now I've laid the groundwork the rest'll make more sense.

You must have had one of those relationships you know isn't right and won't last. When you know darn fine there's a better one out there but you just haven't found it yet. I used to think of those relationships as stops on a train journey. I might get out, wander around, see the local sights. Soon enough I'd be back on that train, going somewhere more important. I always believed I'd reach that special destination; find that other person out there who was travelling from afar to meet me.

Right now I'm seeing Ike Delgado. And because I've run out of track – because the whole world's run out of track – I'm going to be seeing him a lot longer than I'd planned to. For the moment, as far as I can tell, my train ain't leaving this Station.

By a coincidence of some kind, someone coined the name the 'Nielsen and McKinley Station' for this hastily cordoned-off ghetto of ours, this last stop on the line. The block is sandwiched between 33rd and 34th streets going north-south and Nielsen and McKinley going the other way. Mostly, we just call it the Station. I believe we do this in the hope that one day there will be some other place to go, a recommencing of all our broken journeys.

This thing that happened, the day the Long Silence began, we don't know if it was a bomb, something in the water, something they sprayed on us from jets or if it was nature's answer to the craziness of the world. The strange thing was it didn't affect everyone in the city. It was more prevalent among the office workers, pen pushers and keyboard punchers. The class of workers that weren't really working class. Or maybe it was where they were on the day it happened, high up in their office blocks. Whatever the case might be, they're out there, outside our wall, all over this city in their thousands. In their hundreds of thousands. You know them as soon as you see them. We've come to know them as the Commuters because they still get around.

And we're the Stoppers. Because we live in a Station. Because we're going nowhere.

Because we put an end to Commuters.

True, we're not real soldiers but we keep our equipment clean and in good working order nevertheless. Only a suicide wants a gun to jam or misfire when they're crewing. It's best to get outside while it's still light, before the Commuters arrive. Otherwise, they'll be ready for us. About the time the sun gets blocked by the tallest buildings in the city is when we get ready.

To be safe.

It's what we do.

Before we climb the ladder we test our gear one last time. Everyone flicks the miner's lights on their heads to check the batteries. Everyone carries a spare in their pack. We ensure our weapons are fully-loaded, safeties on until we get outside. I carry two pump-action shotguns. Each holds eight rounds. The stocks are plastic so they're lighter for me to carry. Kane is loaded with ordinary scatter-shot cartridges. I have him handy as I exit the cellar. Abel contains cartridges with single slugs. On the rare occasions I draw Abel it's for heavy work. His recoil is so fierce it hurts my shoulder to fire him. In case of emergencies, I carry the paramedic – a .38 snub I use on fellow Stoppers for total anaesthesia. Got snacks and water for later in the shift and a first-aid kit, which if you ask me is a waste of space. Get hurt on the other side of the wall and the chances are you're not coming back to the Station for a change of dressings.

What's a woman doing carrying guns and making out like she's a militiaman?

Surviving.

Just like everyone else.

Chapter Two

Here's how the crew works:

Anyone can volunteer as often as they like. Some put in a request every day, others occasionally. Those who don't want to crew don't get a choice. Once a week, every name goes into the cracker barrel. That makes it fair.

Non-volunteers run the highest risk outside – they haven't built any skills. They don't have knowledge. None of the regulars *want* them on the crew but everyone understands why it's important. It mustn't become a case of us protecting them. We have to work together. Everyone must contribute.

Despite the weekly non-volunteer lottery there are still people who've never taken a gun outside the walls of the Station. People like my man Ike. But that doesn't really matter. The lottery exists to ensure everyone is eligible, even if they haven't had the pleasure.

Seven on the crew again. Seven soldiers. Seven sinners. Seven stars.

It's like a magic formula. Something sacred. The number seven protects us. Sending seven, it takes away the wrongness of what we do. I don't know how we decided on this number or whose idea it was. Like so many important things, it just happened.

Among the seven, I feel safe. As safe as anyone can.

"Everybody ready?"

Monty Spence, tonight's captain, looks from face to face in the restaurant cellar on 33rd. We use different exits each night. Sometimes over the wall, sometimes under it, always a different side of the Station.

Each of us nods. This is the moment, just before we leave the sanctuary of the Station, the threshold moment beyond which nothing is certain. Each of us sits in that cellar wondering if tonight's the night we don't come back. Reaching into a future we haven't the eyes to see. We assess ourselves for 'bad feelings', test our inner winds, watch for signs in everything around us. We're compressed towards this moment like particles in a syringe. There's only one way and that's out.

Spence climbs the ladder, pistols strapped on each side of his chest and a sawn-off slung over his shoulder. He listens through the steel plates that form the cellar doors. These panels are tough, set into the concrete of a once thronging sidewalk. The Commuters will never get through it. Spence keeps us waiting though. He doesn't want to climb into trouble. Neither do we.

My guess is nine out of every ten people in the Station put themselves up for the daily crew lottery. That must seem like craziness but there's something more to it. Most of us had jobs before all this. I used to work as a hairdresser only a couple of blocks away. I spent my days cutting, colouring, bleaching, styling, talking shit to the customers. Can't say I was a big cog in society's machinery but I had my place. After the world went quiet we all lost that sense of who we were. Most of us lost our families and friends – the people who gave us our identities. The world lost its face too. Suddenly it was a place none of us recognised. So we seek order. We impose order. We need to know who we are.

Crewing gives us back a sense of identity and purpose. It's a job every stopper respects, one that most of us want to do. And it must be done.

Spence looks down at us and nods.

He unclasps the padlock.

He pushes open one half of the cellar door. A rope allows him to lower it silently to the surface of the street. He does the same on the other side and steps up into the city night. We wait. A few seconds later he whispers:

"It's clear."

One by one we climb the ladder into the night shift.

We go to work.

No TV or radio. No internet connection. It's been like this from the start.

The same questions occupy us every day. Is anyone else out there? If not in the city then beyond it somewhere? Holed up like us perhaps and struggling to stay alive? I believe it. I believe they're out there but right now it isn't safe to go. We can't walk out of here. We certainly can't drive. Whatever happened that day stopped every car in the city, every wrist watch, every cell phone. Anything with a spark of electricity running through it died and stayed dead.

The only exceptions are simple things like flashlights. Take the flashlight apart, clean its components and put it back together. Bang, it works. Don't ask me why. The one person in the Station who understands what could cause this is Davey Sontaig. He says the only thing that could knock everything out that way is an EMP; some kind of magnetic pulse. It could have been a weapon, he says. Or it could have been a big solar flare. The world's still spinning but it went very quiet that day.

Every once in a while we see a car we haven't tried before and we turn the key. It's like squeezing a pistol trigger and not even hearing a click. Silent and dead. I keep hoping we'll run into some people out there, people like us but with some smarts. People who can get us moving again, get our train out of the Station.

Once we're up, Monty closes the steel doors just as carefully. Below, someone snaps the padlock shut. They'll stay down there all night waiting for us to come back. Whether we're early or late, they'll be there to let us in.

On the sidewalk we spread into a V like flying geese. Monty leads us off into the night. City nights used to be almost as bright as day at street level. Gleams from headlights and shop fronts and streetlamps and neon created electric day when the sun was too tired to continue.

It's different now. You'd expect it to be as dark as a forest on a cloudy night but it isn't. In every street and from every direction comes a kind of light with no obvious source. Its greenish and we see as though through night vision lenses. No one knows where the light comes from but it's another thing we all think about. Some people like to discuss it, others keep their theories to themselves. You can't put all these anomalies together and be glad about what it points to. We're all trying to survive. Thinking about the worst thing that could happen might be realistic but it doesn't do anything for your will to keep fighting. It doesn't help you to stay alive.

Sometimes, though, you can't help thinking about it. It comes over everyone from time to time. That's when the suicides happen. People walking out of the Station alone and unarmed without telling anyone. Then, hours or days later, we realise someone's missing and search the whole Station in case they're sick or there's been an accident. So far it's never been that. It's been someone who's stopped believing in the future and wants to get the waiting over with.

Funny how they never slit their wrists or hang themselves. They always leave the Station. Perhaps they sense they're dishonouring us by dying here when, in their hearts, they're no longer part of the place. Perhaps they're ashamed of giving up. Or maybe, and this is what I believe, they want to see the outside world one last time. They want to walk unimpeded through the streets of the city, make a break for the city limits and try to see some place they've never seen before. I guess if they left early enough they could get out beyond the suburbs and see some open land. Maybe. They'd have to walk hard and fast. Or they'd have to run. Do they just walk to a park bench not far away and imagine the sights and sounds of the city all around them as though it was a perfectly normal day? Maybe they do that instead of waiting for nightfall. One last beautiful day in the city. The way it used to be.

Sometimes I think suicide creeps up on a stopper and they don't even know it. The subconscious tells them their life is over but the conscious mind won't accept it and they just keep fighting on to survive. Stopper's with this problem become machines. When this happens, they can't win. Some deep instinct overcomes everything you thought you believed. An animal in the wild would lie down and die.

Mistakes. That's what gets the subconscious suicides. Accidents. Those are the worst. The ones who believe they're trying to stay alive when deep inside they're already dead. Those are the ones that fight it when the time comes to die. They go the hard way, never giving up.

Makes me sick to think about it.

It's simple, what it all comes down to: get them before they get us.

Do everything we can to make it hard for them, do everything we can to discourage them from coming near us. Reduce them. Cut them down. Course, all we really seem to do is make them desperate, more determined.

I love the daylight in a way I never could before the Long Silence began. The moment I can see without a flashlight or lamp I'm up. It seems safe in the daylight but we're still not certain. Now and then we still lose Stoppers during the day. We just never find out whether they meant to disappear or not.

Chapter Three

As the months pass things do change but never for the better. At first their visits to the Station were sporadic. We blasted them from the walls as they wandered around looking for a way in. The number of visits and the frequency increased. We could hear them outside pounding our walls with their fists, weeping with their heads against shop shutters. It was easy back then. Just lean over the wall, aim and fire.

Did I say easy? I've been here too long.

There's nothing easy about shooting a person. And they still look just like people. They've got their smart suits on or skirts and jackets. They're wearing expensive leather shoes. They look a little untidy, a little unwashed. They stare at you and their eyes plead. They can't speak but they can wail. They can sob. They hold out their hands to you as though they're beggars on the verge of starvation, their faces weaken into looks of privation and their eyes, their lively, imploring eyes impart the deepest sense of utter poverty and need. God, if the world was the way it used to be you'd take them in your arms and hold them tight, give them all the love and money they asked for. But nothing's the way it used to be. If you let them touch you they'll drag you away to wherever it is they hide and you'll come back, mute save for your tears, with that same want in your eyes. So you direct the barrel of a firearm at them, at the heads if you're serious about stopping them looking at you that way. If you're serious about staying alive. If you're a stopper. If you belong on the Kill Crew.

And calm as anything, calm as you can, without blinking at the report or the gun bucking in your grip, you bring the trigger home and release the lead. And the sobbing stops. And you sigh again and again. And maybe you throw up, or, if you can't take in what you've just done, you throw up the second time and the third and the fourth. And often, as you grind your teeth, and the blasting of human heads, the murder of others becomes easier, you find yourself muttering under your breath at the sobbing, plaintive whining, relentless zombies that used to make this city run and you're saying: "Shut up you motherfucker. Shut up motherfucker. Shut up. Shut up. Shut up."

And sometimes you'll mutter the very same thing as you walk around the alleys of the Nielsen and McKinley Station, surrounded by your allies and friends and lovers and acquaintances. And no one will say a word about it to you because everyone understands what you do. You're Kill Crew. Without you the Station dies, too.

Just because it was safe yesterday doesn't mean it will be safe today. Just because they didn't move during daylight yesterday doesn't mean they won't move in it today. We've all got this feeling of progression and development. Almost as though they have some kind of plan. How that can be so when they never speak, I don't understand. But just because they didn't speak today, it doesn't mean they won't speak tomorrow.

One thing we're fairly certain of is their growing numbers. If they're not getting people from us, they must be taking them from somewhere else. That means there are others out there, trying to survive just like we are. So far we haven't gone far enough in a day to find where they are. We're trapped by the length of a day. We can go half a day in any direction as long as we're back by nightfall. But that's not a job for the Kill Crew. That's a job for a search party.

Crewing tonight we have Naomi Birchfield, Winni Grant, Forrest Rubin, Lee Granger, Frieda Hartley, Monty Spence and yours truly, Sheri Foley. More women than men. That's lotteries for you. I'm not complaining; the Long Silence has evened things up between the sexes. Were down to a couple hundred souls. Crewing has become both an obligation and a right.

Up here on the sidewalk it's still dusk but the natural light of day is fading and the unnatural glow of the new nights is overwhelming it. It's like the night doesn't belong to us any more. Like it doesn't even belong to the world any more. This is a night none of us recognise but it's one we're learning to live with.

First task is to trace the edge of the Station, make sure it's clear before we move off. This part is easy. We're within touching distance of safety and other Stoppers are up there on the walls watching over us as we make our circuit. We check for signs of attempted entry, evidence of new methods.

Near a rusted-shut padlock, I find something.

"Fucking freaks. Check this out, Monty."

I hold up splintered fragments.

"Jesus," he says. "That's novel."

The others crowd around my open palm.

"Not too bright, are they?" says Naomi.

The others laugh but it's a little too jolly. Only Monty and I remain serious.

"They don't have to be smart," he says. "Not when they're this determined. What must it take to do something like this?"

"A top dollar dental scheme?" says Naomi. This time we all laugh even though it's not funny that a commuter has tried to bite through a steel lock. It's disturbing. Thinking about the clamping of the jaw and the subsequent failure of dentition, how it must have sounded, how it felt. It makes my skin shrink and pucker.

Winni Grant lays a hand on my shoulder. I guess my disgust must show.

"You okay, Sheri?"

"Fine. We should probably keep moving."

Monty nods and we move off. Five minutes into the shift and already Kane's stock is slithering in my hands. I wipe each hand on the thigh of my jeans as we patrol. It doesn't make any difference. Back in V-formation we head west on McKinley. We work around the abandoned cars but most of them are parked up neatly and the road is pretty clear.

Daylight is all but gone. Now we walk through tenebrous night the colour of bile.

Lee Granger and Forrest Rubin have fallen out of formation. I listen to what they say.

"I'm telling you, Lee, this is caused by radiation of some kind."

"What do you mean?"

"Like those glow in the dark toys they used to put in boxes of cereal. They were radioactive. That's why they don't put them in these days. Stop kids growing a second head or whatever."

"No one's making Count Chocula any more, Forrest."

"You know what I'm saying."

"Okay, so where did this radiation come from?"

"I think it was a bomb, some kind of weapon."

"Yeah? So where's the invasion force?"

"Are you serious?"

"Sure. There should have been brigades of enemy troops here by now. There's nothing."

"Shit, Lee. Grow a fucking brain here, man. The Commuters are the invaders. The first wave, at least."

"No. They were already here."

"Exactly. What could be smarter than that? Turn the enemy population against itself. Make everyone crazy and let your target country melt down from the inside. Then, when there's no one left to fight you, that's when you move in. I think we're just waiting for the second wave. One night we'll be out here crewing and we'll run into some real fucking soldiers. That'll be our last turkey shoot, right there."

Forrest's theory isn't watertight. None of the theories are. Still, it's given Lee something to think about. Apparently Lee Granger can't think and talk at the same time and for that I'm glad. I like a silent shift. That way, I know everyone's concentrating on the job.

Even though my palms are sweating, I'm shivering. I don't know why but I'm not feeling the pulse tonight, I don't have my inner rhythm. I'm having problems keeping my mind on what's out here in front of me even though my eyes flick from side to side and I can't think about anything else but where we're going to find Commuters. Something's not right and suddenly I'm wondering, is this what it means to get a bad feeling? And I think; has part of me died already? Is this my last trip out on the crew?

Up ahead, Monty holds up a hand and we halt. It's early to be seeing Commuters this close to the Station so maybe it's nothing. Or maybe it's just a cat chasing a rat between the dumpsters in an alley. None of the animals seem to be affected. Monty doesn't move. Fingers click safeties off. Seven people hear nothing but their breathing and heartbeat in a deserted, night time city street. I've stopped counting how many times I've done this. Even in this partial light, I can see Frieda Hartley trembling. I'd put a hand out to steady her if I didn't think the shock of my touch would make her swing round and shoot me. Frieda's a non-volunteer. This is her second shift on the crew so she already knows how bad it's going to be.

We wait.

I can't tell why Monty hasn't moved on until I see the silhouetted group of Commuters stepping out from both sides of the street. He's shocked because this is different behaviour. Not smart necessarily, but organised. Premeditated. The Commuters have been waiting for us. Maybe they even placed themselves here last night so that they'd be ready for us when we arrived.

Monty gives a signal for us to spread out across the street. He won't let us shoot yet because there's no point in wounding them. It just makes them mad. You have to wait until you're clear for a head shot. When they're in range, he'll let us fire at will.

But if they were waiting for us, how did they know which route we'd take from the Station? The answer is they couldn't possibly know. All they could do was wait in every street. I don't want to turn around because I know what I'm going to see.

Frieda turns her face towards me, looking for some kind of reassurance, I guess. I go to her and whisper what I believe are the words she needs to hear.

"Do not be afraid. Be efficient. Be a surgeon. Stay calm and stay next to me. Okay?"

She nods, eyes staring.

But she's not staring at me. She looking at what's behind me and now I have to turn around.

Commuters. Dozens of them. Converging on us.

There's no point sneaking around any more.

"Monty," I say and he turns, angry until he sees what I've seen.

His decision is instant and unprecedented.

"Fall back to the Station. Stay together. Take as many as you can."

"Can we shoot them yet?" asks Frieda.

I giggle. I don't know why.

"Fuck yes," says Monty.

And hot lead erupts into the street.

Chapter Four

Seven's always been enough. Even when things go wrong.

Tonight, seven is not a magic number.

We walk – we do not run – east, back to the Station. I must have been deep in thought because we've come a lot farther than I realised. We reform the V but now I'm on point and Monty's on my right tail. Frieda's right beside me, too fucking close really but it's my own fault for telling her what I did. Commuters close in from both sides and we dispatch them as soon as they're close enough.

Here comes a typical suit from my left. Some guy with duck's disease – his ass is too close to his feet. A paisley tie – hard to tell if it's silk in this gloom – and tassled leather piss-catchers on his feet. No style. Probably a fucking accountant. He looks miserable enough. I shoulder Kane and pop the guy's noodle from ten feet. Ten feet is not a long way. It's three steps. Maybe four for a short-ass commuter like this one. He doesn't take any more steps. Usually there's time to watch them collapse to the street. Never happens the same way twice, and, as sick as it makes me to kill anything, even these wailing bags of bones, I like to watch that shit. There's unique poetry in the way a body falls. Like throwing I-Ching coins or something. Therein you could see your future. I can't get enough of that shit.

But not tonight. It's way too busy. Already some PA type chick with her hair up and still wearing her glasses after all these months totters towards me on heels that could be weapons. I pump Kane up. He blows. She goes down. Finally messy and dishevelled. I pump again. Guy with no jacket or tie, shirt open at the neck. Must have been at lunch when his world ended. Now it ends again.

To my right, I can hear Frieda firing too many shots too close together. She's missing heads with more than half of them, so now there's half shot Commuters screaming in pain and desperation and still after her along with all the others. If they take her, it'll be me next. I've got a few seconds so I reload Kane and take out four of Frieda's new friends. But by now, I'm angry.

"You calm the fuck down, lady," I shout. "You wait until they are in range. You aim carefully and only when you are sure will you fire. Do you understand?"

"I know, I know. I'm sorry." She's crying so hard she can barely see through the tears, barely hold her weapon steady over her spasming solar plexus.

"Don't be sorry, Frieda. Be precise. Then maybe we'll all get home."

Course my side's filled up again and aim-boom, aim-boom, aim-boom, aim-boom

The way is clear.

Kane is hot now. Hotter than he wants or ought to be. I don't know how many more shots he's got before he's more of a danger to me than the Commuters. Still, I reload - no choice - and burn my knuckles on his sleek, black barrel. I'm not used to this intensity though and out of the corner of my eye I see some CEO type in an Italian suit that fits like he was born in it. He's got slicked back hair and for all I know he styled it before he came out. I fumble the last shell into Kane's hungry breech but the CEO's got his arms out and he's got a hold of my hair before I can pump.

Jesus, I think, this really is my last trip out. The beginning of my new 'life' with the Commuters, a life of purest lack. To the sound of a bomb going off, the CEO's head disappears. Lee Granger's fired his gun right beside my ear. I don't hear myself say, "Thanks, Lee." And there's no time to see if he even heard me. I drop two more Commuters and then there's a lull.

I check behind and I'm relieved to see we're all still here. Not the neatest formation but not a pack running scared either. Even Frieda seems to have taken a hold of herself. I sling Kane over my shoulder and hope he doesn't melt his sheath. Now it's Abel's turn and that means everybody gets hurt. Because of his stallion-like kick, that includes me.

Monty shouts:

"They're thinning out. Keep moving. We're halfway there."

I've never heard him so breathless.

You don't fire Abel from the hip if you still want to be holding a shotgun after the fact. Abel belongs tightly drawn in to the shoulder. A shot from Abel doesn't scatter so it's worth using the sights. In this way, you're assured of a bruised cheekbone and raw collarbone. The pain, swelling and stiffness can last for ten days. I assume if I keep doing it I'll develop some kind of repetitive strain injury. Already I have problems uncurling my trigger finger for several hours following a shift on the crew. All this beats being dragged into the unknown by the Commuters.

At least, I think it does. You've never seen such miserable looking individuals in your life. Lamenting some forgone thing none of us can define. Maybe it's their souls if that isn't too religious a take on the whole thing. Maybe they're in some kind of pain and we're the antidote to it. Maybe they're being controlled by some outside force none of us are aware of yet. Who the hell knows? But am I being too narrow minded here? Could it be that being a commuter only looks bad from the outside? The motherfuckers may have attained nirvana for all I know. Maybe we're the freaks; the Stoppers. Maybe we're the aberrations and we don't even know it. Maybe we're the enemy.

It doesn't pay to think like this too long or too often. That's when the siren voice of suicide begins to lull you, send you to a long and early sleep.

The antidote is a night crewing.

See me. A woman. Carrying not one but three firearms and other lethal weapons I haven't mentioned. How the hell could that happen, you ask? Everything I've been telling you, that's how. And I'll tell you something else. Blowing away some whingeing deadbeat suit with a single blast from a pump-action shotgun goes a long way towards easing my PMS.

"Oh, you like hard candy? Suck on this."

Watching a baseball-sized hole open up in this commuter's head is almost enough to stop me feeling Abel's angry kick. Almost.

The Commuters have thinned out. The Station is a few yards away. Soon we'll all be firing backwards to save our asses until we get back in.

Monty's shouting:

"Drop the ladders! We're coming over."

Faces appear at the crest of the nearest part of the wall. The faces of friends, survivors. The last humans alive for all we know. This is our family now, the Stoppers that hold out in the Nielsen and McKinley Station. Aluminium ladders with hooks at the top appear over the wall. At the top of each one two Stoppers, each armed with their favourite tools, wait. No more Commuters stand between us and the wall. I reload, turn and back away from the creatures of the city night, firing when necessary. Then my back is touching cold metal and then I'm climbing without looking back. From above, shots roast the air on either side of me but I'm glad. While that lead rains down, nothing can touch us.

There's a scream behind me and I stop to look down. Three Commuters have taken hold of Frieda. She's trying to reload her gun but she's spilling every cartridge onto the sidewalk because she's trying to struggle away from them at the same time.

Someone's shouting:

"Reload and fire, Frieda. They won't let go otherwise."

I realise it's my voice.

I see myself climbing back down the ladder.

Everyone else is already on the ascent, thank God, but Monty's not pleased.

"Sheri, get back up here now."

"I'm not leaving her."

"It's her own goddamned fault."

I'm still descending the ladder.

"It's only her second shift, Monty."

"You're putting yourself at unnecessary risk."

I'd stop and bawl him out if there was time, tell him that risk is all we have left, all we know, and all we live for in this new world we call the Station. But I can't spare the breath or the time to reply. Instead I'm talking to Frieda. It's a bad scene. There are four of them on her now and more moving in from every direction.

"Load your gun, babe. I'm right with you."

Abel is fully loaded. I aim and take down some yuppie with a ponytail. A fraction to the right some office junior ignores the danger he's in the way all of them do. He looks a lot more junior without his head. Now Frieda's right arm is free and some steel has come to her hand. I see her fit two, wait, three cartridges into her shotgun. It's enough. She steers the barrel under the chin of some drippy, wet nosed secretarial type and makes a big mess. Gasping through a mask of hot gore she turns to the final commuter but he turns with her. I aim but can't fire because I could just as easily hit her now they're moving so much. A hand takes hold of my shoulder. Without even looking I bring the butt up and stab it backwards, this gives me long enough to turn and decapitate my suited assailant with a single shot.

Frieda's waltz with her last determined abductor has become frantic.

"Get the fuck off me you piece of scum."

I've never heard Frieda swear before. If she makes it through this she'll be a changed woman. Believe me, I know.

"Forget his head. Shoot his leg out."

She nods, teeth showing, points the shotgun down and kneecaps the commuter. The dance ends. I pull Abel tight and the commuter's head evaporates. Frieda's a real mess now.

"Reload and run, babe. We're going home."

"I'm out."

"Shit. Take these."

I hold out five cartridges. Her hands are iron-steady. She focusses like some kind of silently chanting priest as she counts the cartridges into the breech. Like I said, a changed woman. Side by side we lope back to the wall. It's farther away than I thought but it's makeable. Easily makeable.

"Sheri!"

I don't know where my concentration was for just that one second. To my left there's a group of Commuters coming in really fast. Sprinting. I don't remember seeing them move like that before. They look like…like a pack. I've already made the necessary mental calculations. We don't have enough shots to take them all down. We can fire but we have to make to the wall. We have to *race* the fuckers.

"Just run," I scream. "Get to the ladders."

Monty and the rest of the crew are up there now and their faces remind me of the Commuters so much because they believe they are about to lose something precious. Isn't that a nice thought? That we are a part of them they don't want to be without? Take it forward a few months when the numbers are down still more. Each one of us that doesn't make it back brings the rest closer to the end. The end we've all begun to believe is inevitable. Their expressions change, worsen. Hands are lifting to cover mouths. As they do I hear the sound of a shotgun clattering to the road and skittering away. Frieda has tripped. She is falling. Her hands are held out in front to protect herself. I gauge the distance between this new mob of running Commuters and us and the distance between us and the wall. We can still do it but she has to land well and rise quickly for it to be possible. I realise, as a manic, half-laugh escapes me, that this is the worst shift I've been on. Ever.

Frieda falls, rolls and stands again. Like a stuntwoman. I could kiss her.

But then I see she can't run any more. Her left foot is hanging at a strange ankle. She hops onwards but she's falling back. The Commuters change course. They don't want us any more. They want her.

I should keep running. I've watched her ass all night. I've been back once for her already. Once more than anyone else would have. She's grunting against the pain and pushing herself on. She's acting like someone who wants to live. And I decide then: Frieda is not a suicide. She's a survivor. Like me, before I crewed, she just hasn't developed the stomach for violence yet. I turn back and our eyes meet.

She sees me. She sees the wall behind me. She sees the pack of racing Commuters and many more coming from beyond. She stops hopping. It's like someone switched off the power to a remote control robot. She shakes her head at me, almost shrugging with her eyes. Now Frieda is not going to make it. She ain't never coming back.

The pack slam into her and they all go down. There's still time.

I draw the paramedic from my boot and walk calmly to the downed scrum of bodies. Frieda's face is pale in the green glow of the city's unnatural night as the Commuters maul her, try to haul her in several directions at once. She looks desperate, impatient.

I aim between her eyes, where they shoot horses.

And then I run. Like a survivor. Like a person who wants to stay alive.

"What the fuck did you think you were doing out there?"

I don't answer. Can't.

Monty paces the cellar pushing clawed fingers through his thinning hair again and again. The rest of the crew has been dismissed. He doesn't want anyone else to hear this. That's why we're sitting back in the basement where we started out. I don't know what time it is but it must be long after midnight. We've been sitting here in silence a long time already. Maybe Monty was waiting for me to say something first. Or maybe he just couldn't think how to begin. Now he has. But I don't feel like I ever want to speak again.

"No one goes back, Sheri. Ever. You know that."

He's stopped pacing now and he's eyeballing me but I'm staring through some gritty patch of basement floor. My mind's a jungle of movement but my body's a piece of stone. Maybe this is how catatonics feel. Alive within a motionless carapace. Monty reaches into one of the many pockets of a Banana Republic reporter's jacket. Most of the pockets are full of shells. This is ammo of a different sort.

He taps a Marlboro from the soft pack, holds it out. I could start smoking, I suppose, but I refuse.

"Tell me what happened, Sheri. Tell me what went through your mind. I need to know what's going on inside you. You're old school as far as this thing goes, an elder of the crew, if you will. People look up to you whether you know it or not. They respect you. If you start taking risks, they will too. That means we lose, Sheri. It means we lose quick. And if they don't think it was bravery that motivated you, they'll think you're a suicide and that's worse."

I'm able to meet his gaze now but still no words come.

"See, I can understand your thinking. Rather, I can understand thought had nothing to do with it. It's where we all fall down. All of us. Even me. We're not soldiers. We don't have that discipline, that detachment, that remote control conditioning that makes us do things by the numbers out there. What we need are some fucking marines up in here. Not just to do the crewing but to teach us how to do it properly."

He smokes for a while. Less tense it seems.

"In the old world. In the old city what you did tonight would mark you out as a hero, Sheri. Not only that, you acted out of utterly selfless compassion for another human being. You put your life at risk to save Frieda Hartley. It was the action of a saint."

He takes a big drag on his Marlboro, deflating its cylindrical skin, drawing a too-long red tip on it. He drops the butt to the damp, macular ground and crushes it under his boot. Then, he breathes out a mist of judgement and speaks for the last time tonight.

"I love you, Sheri. I love you like my own child. But I'm standing here to tell you you can never do that again. If I think you're going to behave that way on my shift, if I get an inkling that you're wigging out, if I think you look distracted or anything other than focussed on wiping out Commuters, I will not allow you to crew again. Once I make that decision, I won't unmake it. Do you understand what I'm telling you?"

I really do feel like a sullen teenager. Is that just because we all step into the nearest, most appropriate roles for us? Is it because I miss my dad?

I stand up from the crate that's been turning my ass into a waffle and place myself a foot in front of Montgomery Wichita Spence. I look him in the eye and fold him in half with my fist. For years I've been practising Bruce Lee's one-inch-punch. I can't do it with one inch but I can do it with six. While he struggles for breath, I leave.

Some nights, I'm just not in the mood for conversation.

Trixie rolls a double six and moves four white counters six spaces before scooping her ivory dice back into their fur-lined leather shaker. She's a lucky girl but not as lucky as me. Right now I'm letting her win because I'm playing right-handed. I shake with my right hand, move the counters with my right hand. Playing this way leaves me vulnerable to the whims of the universe. When it comes to backgammon, I can survive a little rotten luck. Especially if it means seeing Trixie jump around like she's queen of the city. If I play left-handed, I never lose. I get the numbers that stack my counters up like the walls of the Station. I get doubles ad infinitum. I land on every unguarded enemy counter. Usually, I save my left hand for playing Ike. He hates to lose.

"Nice tricks, Trix," I say after her double sixes.

She sticks out her tongue. I'm the only one who calls her Trix. I'm one of the only ones she talks to even after all these months. Still, she doesn't say much. We communicate by implication much of the time. By reading each other's auras. By passing time together.

I roll three and four from my right hand. My counters are a mess, no formation, singles left unmarked. Trixie takes full advantage on her next turn sending two of my counters off the board. Already she's getting her counters home and out. Looks like I'll still have some in the starting box.

Ten rolls later and the game is hers.

She leaps up and does her victory dance. I don't think anyone else in the Station has seen her this uninhibited. All of us are damaged but Trixie's damage tore off her old skin and now she's someone new. Someone I allow myself to be with without knowing. Do you think perhaps that's how we all are with each other, how we always were before all this? Did anyone really know anyone else or did they just pretend to because it made them feel better than admitting they understood nothing of each other?

Trixie is an island and there are no maps to tell you where her active volcanoes are situated, where her unpolluted streams are, her quicksand, her tribes of hungry cannibals.

She sits down on a bean bag with a heavy flump. I swear she does this because she wants to see if she can burst it. One day I think she may succeed. I won't bawl her out over it. Probably we'll both fall around laughing until one of us starts to cry. We'll cry because nothing matters any more. Not true, we'll cry because some things don't matter any more and others matter more than ever. The rules are all different. We don't yet understand this new world.

Her words, coming as they do from a planet of mostly silent gestures, startle me.

"Why don't the other women talk to you, Sheri Foley?"

And then their meaning startles me worse. What do I say to her? Because I can shoot a gun and fight better than most men in the Station? Because they think I'll try and munch their rugs? Because I have a wounded heart and tongue like a bullwhip? Trixie's just a girl. No, forget I said that. This world has no children, no matter how poor in years a soul may be. Still, what do I tell her? She's taken a risk. Come out of verbal hiding in order to pose a question. Maybe she's been thinking about it for weeks.

Maybe months.

I take a breath to reply. I really do want to try and explain. But there's a problem. Three little words that have replaced the ones we all used to be so fond of. So I tell her that instead:

"I don't know."

She is very still for a long time. Far longer than any child ought to be capable of. Then she yawns and struggles out of the bean bag. She reaches a hand out to me and I struggle out of mine. We leave the backgammon set as it is, a battleground where the recent victory is still very obvious. In the old world I could never have afforded an item like this. Mine would have been plastic and cardboard, not ebony, ivory, oak, fur and leather. But it might as well be plastic and cardboard for these things no longer matter to us. Trixie leads me to my bedroom and, still yawning, strips down to her vest and pants.

She has tiny points of nipple under which breasts have been willed to her, yet to be bequeathed. A suggestion of filamental hair has taken root under her arms and down covers her legs from ankle to groin. She is straight, going to be very tall if she lives that long, but has no curves yet to speak of. She is eleven years old. It won't be long now. She sits down on the bed with a bounce and collapses into it as though she's been running up and down hills all day.

I wish I could say she reminds me of me when I was eleven but she doesn't. I was shorter, later in developing, happier, stupider.

I strip off and put on a long tee shirt but I keep my pants on.

I slip into bed beside her and she snuggles back towards me, hauls my arm over her and nestles, hiding from the day world. I'm a lot more comfortable when Trixie stays with me than when I stay with Ike or when he stays here. I feel at peace. Only months before now a grown woman sleeping with a child this age would have been seen as deviant behaviour, verging on the criminal. Some kind of abuse. Now it is absolutely and unequivocally necessary.

Because our time is ending. Because this contact is all we have.

As peaceful as I am, sleep is a long time coming. Trixie sleeps the moment her eyes are closed but in this surrender of her conscious mind she is paying a price I may never understand. Already her eyes are screwing up and her face is twisting into one of its many expressions of terror and abandonment. She will dream this way all night or all day and wake looking more tired than when she went to sleep.

I hold her tight and still I am afraid. I hold her tight because I am afraid.

Chapter Five

Money has no value here any more. We share most of the stuff we find and if we come across something particularly special we keep it for ourselves. No one cares. There's plenty to go round. A whole city's worth of stuff between a couple hundred people.

Day shifts are different. There's no Kill Crew out there. No Commuters. There are three rules you can break at your own peril: one, you don't leave the Station alone. Two, you don't leave the Station unarmed. Three, you always tell someone you're going out. There's an unspoken rule too, if you bring stuff back, bring it for everyone not just for yourself. For the good of the Station. For the good of the Stoppers. Got our own little communist kibbutz going here, I swear.

Today I'm taking Trixie out. She says she wants some new games to play but I plan to walk her way the hell away from the Station. Far enough that she can forget about it for a few hours. Maybe in the rhythm of our footsteps on the deserted streets she'll find a way to talk to me. I can only hope for that. I can't make it happen. This girl needs healing and I wish I could be the channel for it. I have to accept it could be my wishing that's stopping the healing from coming. Sometimes I wonder if I'm really any help to Trixie. If I'm any good to her at all.

I'm pulling my boots on when there's a knock at my apartment door. Rap-tappa-rap.

Shit.

"What is it?"

"It's me. Can I come in?"

"I know *who* it is, Ike. What do you want?"

"Uh…neighbourly visit? Pizza delivery? FBI? Whatever opens the door."

"I'm not dressed yet," I say as I lace up my left combat boot.

"I can wait."

And he will too. That man's got way too much patience. It's unattractive.

In the living room, Trixie's ready. She's been up and ready for an hour or more. I study her face without staring and I see she's unconcerned about Ike. Is she unconcerned that he's outside the door? Unconcerned that he might want to come with us when he finds out what we're doing? Or deliberately unconcerned?

I take my time slipping on my other boot, remove the lace and replace it twice before tying it tight and double. As I walk to the door, Trixie puts away the backgammon as though she's stacking gold coins.

"Hey, Ike."

"Morning."

He's smiling. Unharmed by waiting, Ike seems to expand when he sees me. I turn and walk away before he tries to lay a kiss on me but when I turn around he hasn't moved.

"So, can I come in? I could come back later if you two are busy."

I stand with my arms folded.

"Are you going to tell me what you want?"

Ike's gentle eyes harden over and I realise I'm being inappropriately bitchy. I don't even know why. Under his gaze I'm regretting my attitude but I won't let him see that. He looks like he's going to say something, you know, politely remind me that we're sleeping together, going steady, going steadily nowhere, but whatever that thing is, he doesn't say it. He says:

"I was really sorry to hear about Frieda. I know this isn't the time but if ever you do want to talk about it, Sheri, well…you know what I'm saying."

Trixie looks from his face to mine watching every unspoken communication, every buried gesture and emotion. I wish she wouldn't do that. She doesn't need to know about this stuff. She's too young. Then I remind myself that Trixie has seen far worse than this when she was younger than she is now. Who am I to say what she does or doesn't need? And Ike's patient, caring blankness is driving me nuts. He's got no fucking personality at all.

"Yeah. Okay. Thanks."

Three little words. More than he deserves.

"You two getting ready to go out?"

I shrug like we might or might not. Like, who cares anyway?

"Can I tag along?"

Tag along? He must know it's the most lame thing he could have said. The wimpiest way of asking to accompany us he could have dreamed up. He does know. I can see a little burn creeping from his neck to his cheeks. His stature deflates. For a moment I'm happy. I could almost smile.

"This is a ladies day out."

"Okay. But…I mean, will you be…safe?"

"It's daylight, Ike."

"Sure it is…but–"

I could laugh now. The idea that we need to be accompanied. Protected by Isaac Delgado.

"If it wasn't safe out there, Ike, what good would it do for you to be with us? Can you even fire a gun?"

He shakes his head. The embarrassment, if that's what it was, is gone.

"I just hate the thought of you being out there. I hate the thought of–"

"It's fine with me," says Trixie like she's the world's greatest conversationalist. Like she's some kind of goddamned social secretary. And then, as though this is nothing more than a shopping trip, she says. "We can bring back more stuff."

Ike's blinking. I'm unable to speak. I'd like to take Trixie into the other room and chew her ear off. No, I'd like to paddle her meddlesome ass. Our ladies day out is history. The channelling of much needed healing will have to wait for a manless day. God knows when that will be. Although, you could argue that even with Ike there it'll still be a manless day.

"Fine," I say. "Tag along if you want. But you're taking a gun. And you're taking a cart too."

I stomp towards the door and he gets out of the way just in time to avoid getting flattened.

Ike Delgado. Just a stop on my journey but the fucking train's broken down. No one knows if it'll ever get going again. What pisses me off more than anything is the knowledge that a couple of days into my period, I'll suddenly get over hating everything about Ike Delgado and I'll stay that way for almost three weeks.

This anger, this conflict. It isn't really even me. Is it? Can I be permanently defined by what I am for only five or six days out of every month?

You're fucking right I can.

Three miles out from the Station and not a single word has passed between us. If it had been just me and Trixie, that's what I would have expected. With the three of us it's different. There's no point in pretending none of us know what this looks like: Mummy, Daddy and daughter. But even Ike, who wanted so much either to be with us or not to be left behind at the Station, even Ike is uncomfortable now that he's here. Like me he wears his shotgun in a sling over his shoulder but unlike me he looks like he's wearing a banana back there, not a lethal weapon.

Out of nowhere, Ike starts singing:

"In a town where I was born, lived a man who sailed to sea. And he told me of his life in the land of submarines…"

Trixie looks at him. She looks shocked. But he doesn't stop.

"We all live in a yellow submarine, yellow submarine, yellow submarine. We all live in–"

"Ike."

"What?"

"Don't."

"Am I off key?"

I use my eyes to point to Trixie. I expect him to shut up now but he doesn't. Far from it.

"Hey, Trixie," he says. "Does my singing bother you?"

She looks away and doesn't say anything. I already know she's not going to say anything and I give him a silent I-told-you-so. She probably won't speak for the whole of the day. If he hadn't been here, she might have. I'm thinking about turning back when she says:

"Did you make up those words?"

"No. I wish I had."

"What about the tune? Did you invent it?"

"Huh uh. It's an old song. A song from just before I was born. Do you like it?"

She nods. And then she does something I hardly ever see her do. She smiles.

"I've seen submarines on TV," she says. And then she stops walking. We all stop. "I feel like we really are living in a submarine. Taking a walk like this, it's like being deep sea divers, isn't it?"

"It's exactly like that," says Ike. Me, I don't know what to say. I keep my mouth shut for once.

"Do you think…"

She seems to lose confidence now. Like she's already risked too much.

"Do I think what?" asks Ike.

She looks up at him.

"Do you think they knew? The ones who wrote the song. Do you think they knew this would happen one day and they wrote the song so that we would know someone else understood what it was like to be here? To be like this?"

Ike goes down on one knee and now he's the same size as Trixie. He's going to fuck this up badly.

"Do you like the song?"

She nods. Smiles again.

"Do you like music?"

She shrugs.

"I don't know. I never heard much of it."

"Well, you're right in a way to ask the question. See, music is kind of a language and it's a language that can speak to anyone, anywhere. Even any time. So, even though the people who wrote Yellow Submarine wrote it more than forty years ago, the song still speaks to us now. Even in these strange times. That means they were great musicians. Great communicators. Geniuses."

"What were they called?"

"The Beatles."

"The beetles?"

"Yeah."

A third smile from Trixie makes it a very special day.

"That's a really lame-assed name."

We reach the memorial park. It's a huge parallelogram right in the centre of the city, big enough that some of the main roads go right through it instead of around the outside. From here we can find the department store I have in mind for Trixie's game raid, a place called Loopy's. They were the place to buy stuff for kids before Toys 'r' Us came along. After we get the games, the same street will take us out to the suburbs and beyond if we have the time and the legs to try it.

The grass in the park is brown. Not dead but not right either. The shrubs and trees have a similar look to them, like they're hanging on through some kind of blight or drought. The thing is, there is no drought. It rains just as much now as it ever did. We skirt around the edge of the park because who wants to walk through brown vegetation? I feel like we'd be walking through something dead. Except I know the park is still alive. This is going to sound unhinged but I don't think I'd feel safe in there. What if the stuff in the plants gets into me? I start to think the park is very much the opposite of dead. It lives, it thinks, it observes. I don't want to go in there.

All is silence again between the three of us but it's a good silence now, a silence we can all trust and rely on. It's like a balloon we're all leaning against from different directions. It holds us up and it holds us together.

Outside Loopy's Ike surprises me.

"I'm gonna stay out here while you get what you need. Just keep an eye, you know?"

"There's nothing out here to keep an eye on, Ike."

"Yeah. I know. I'll be right here when you come back. Take as long as you want."

Is that disappointment in Trixie's eyes? I don't believe what's happening here. We push our two carts through the big, glass front doors and Ike leans against the wall. I just hear the rasp of a lighter as the doors shut behind us. He should know better. Smoking kills. It's a bad example for Trixie.

Inside, without power for the fluorescent lighting, it's gloomy. There's a minute film of dust over everything now. All that bright plastic and cellophane, all those colourful enticements and excitements are dull and purposeless. Who will use these toys and games now? Who will ride the scooters, skateboards and BMX bikes? Who will dress up as knights or witches? Who will spend hours leading Lara Croft to treasure through ancient ruins?

I realise I've come to a stop. Staring at all the displays and unopened boxes stacked on the shelves, I'm standing like a mannequin abandoned in the wrong shop. Up ahead Trixie looks back. She doesn't speak, she beckons. And then she smiles – in reassurance – this is getting to be a habit.

A slender man leans against the bricks of a wall. His right hand brings a cigarette to his mouth, lingers and drops away. The hand is long-fingered, artistic. A long panatela would suit it better than a butt. After too long, the man exhales. There's no wind. Somewhere in front of him the smoke evaporates.

Around him rise the blocks of the city. A city built on money, trade and power. A city its dwellers were proud of. A city to be envied. His place in it has changed. He is an ant among tombstones, his colony almost destroyed.

He looks around and he is glad, thankful for the silence. He could never have dreamed such a silence possible, did not even know he wanted it until it surrounded him.

He smokes and listens to the silence.

There must be a tune in his head, for soon he's tapping a rhythm with his boot and drumming his fingers on his thighs, still leaning against the wall. He begins to scan the street, its shop fronts and doorways and second floor windows. When there were people here, this single street would have been home to a thousand secret acts, a million secret thoughts every day. Stories. It would have been full of stories. Now all the stories have gone.

His eyes flicker across the street's facades and he knows that's what they always were. How the street looked and how it actually was were two very different things, things not necessarily related. And the people who once crowded this street buying, selling, walking, driving, hustling, merely passing by, they were the same. They were constructions built to withstand the city but never strong enough to display the truth through undraped windows. What about now? Was it any different in his dwindling colony? He thought not. The buildings were different but the windows remained curtained or shuttered and inside, deep in the cellars and high in the dusty attics, truth still hid. The man expected that was where it would remain until it died.

The city was better in silence for in silence no lies could be told. Nor could brave attempts to tell the truth fail.

Something takes the man's attention more specifically. A large white car parked like all the others. It doesn't belong in the scene. The other cars on the street are saloons and sports cars and practical run-arounds designed for city traffic. They are city-slab shades in the main – grey, gunmetal, black, blue, brown – with only occasional flourishes of colour. But this car is the only white vehicle in the street as far as the man can look in either direction.

It is also larger than most of the other cars because it is not meant for city use. This is a car that would transport tribal warriors across Afghanistan, or insurgents with rocket propelled grenades across a desert. It was a truck really. High suspension, tyres so knobbly they'd grab the dirt, a huge covered bed for equipment in the back. Four doors. Bull bars like iron gates protecting the grille. There wasn't a speck of dirt on the car, nor, he noticed, was there a license plate.

The man had never needed a car in the city and, even if he had, he couldn't have afforded to run one. Now, if he wanted, he could at least find out what it felt like to sit in one. What the hell. Half embarrassed even though there was no one around to see him and grinning like a kid on Christmas morning, he crosses the street, still looking around to see if anyone's watching even though there is no anyone any more.

The closer he gets to the truck the bigger it is. When he gets to it, it towers above him. He stops beside the Hilux feeling a thrill of guilt and even though he tells himself not to be so goddamned stupid, the feeling doesn't go away. He's pleased. He reaches for the door handle, presses the button and pulls. The door opens. It's a big step up to the driver's seat but there's a big step to help him get there. He pulls himself inside, shifts in the seat and pulls the door shut. The car smells brand new and synthetic inside. Maybe it smells of some kind of adhesive, he's not sure. He alters the distance of the seat from the wheel, adjusts the angle of the backrest and places both hands on the steering wheel.

From his high place he looks down on all the other vehicles.

He imagines himself not in the city, dominating other drivers, but out on a highway heading for a county road and from there a dirt road and from there a track until finally he comes to a stone farmhouse very far from the city, very far from anywhere. This is where he'd really like to be. Away from Commuters and Stoppers alike. Somewhere quiet but in a different way to the quiet of the city. Maybe there would be animals out there, animals wild but normal. Maybe the trees out there would be green and spreading and healthy like the trees in the park used to be only bigger, better, more beautiful. The kinds of trees you could build a little tree house in.

And here he stops himself from imagining any more.

His hands fall limp from the steering wheel to rest either side of his lap. All the strength has gone out of them. Ahead all he sees is the dead city in all its abandonment. The imagination is dangerous. There is a difference between hope and illusion. That difference must be respected because within it worms the root of suicide.

The man looks across the street at the shop where the girl and the woman will be exploring, taking clever items from the shelves, items that wear away time and induce momentary forgetfulness of reality. More lies spreading from the old world into the new. For there is no barrier against untruth. It is a disease all are born with, one the man knows he carries just like everyone else. No cataclysm will eradicate it, there is no cure for lies and he is full of them.

The man notices the keys are in the ignition and, because he can't think of anything else to do while he waits, he turns them.

The Hilux grumbles to life at the touch of his slim fingers.

Chapter Six

Trixie's shopping cart is piled high. In it she has placed three two-thousand-piece jigsaws. Stacked beside them is Monopoly, Cleudo, Mousetrap, chess and battleships – all deluxe editions. She has puzzle books by the dozen, especially word-searches and logic problems. There's a jump rope and cabbage patch doll, a Sea Monkey kingdom with years of food supply.

My cart is empty. If there was a firearm department in this store, I'd be looking at the guns, filling the cart with ammo. I would feel as though I were stealing gold bars. But there's no gun counter here. Maybe there'll be time for that later.

The only noise as we survey the aisles is the rubbery squeak of our boots on the waxy floor and the occasional cage-rattle of something being dumped into my cart now that Trixie's is full. We'll share some of the stuff out back at the Station. I wonder how we'll feel using all these things. Do we still understand about fun? Can there be anything more to these games other than merely passing our trapped time?

My stomach rumbles. I haven't eaten anything interesting for weeks and weeks. Somewhere on this street is a deli, I seem to remember. There's more growling inside as I think about what we might find.

"Hey, Trixie, I'd like to get out of here now. There's some other places I'd like to go before we head back."

Trixie looks over her shoulder at me and then into her cart.

"Did I take too much stuff?"

"No, honey. But we'll need a little space in case we find some other good things. Come on, let's get going."

We haven't gone up to the next floor – all electronic and computer stuff that's useless now – or the floor above that for every kind of sports equipment. There'll be another day and Trixie's mature enough to realise it. I even think she's beginning to understand the need for delaying gratification.

It's as we approach the front door to leave that we both hear a sound like a cough and we stop to listen because we both know that's not what it is. The cough becomes a confident rumble then three higher-pitched whines. Just as unexpectedly, the sound stops.

We're both running, carts forgotten behind us.

Coming back to the Station is one of the hardest things I've ever done. I thought I knew what it meant to be conflicted because of my relationship with Ike. Just goes to show how a wrong a person can be.

All the various theories the Stoppers have about what's really going on, they represent the natural craving for knowledge and answers that humans have always displayed. The thing about knowledge is you can't unknow it. Finding answers isn't always what you hope it will be. Especially when the answers aren't the ones you'd wished for. The three of us return to the Station with knowledge. Some is good. Some is not.

On the way back we pass by the park and I stop to study the things that still grow there. I stop for a long time. There's something in there, something good I'm hoping, that may take away some of my unease. Something from the old world. I almost don't believe it's possible.

"What is it, Sheri?"

Both of them have been watching me stare into the park but it's Ike that gives way to his curiosity. Maybe Trixie is still too overwhelmed by what she's seen to give a shit about my fixation with a patch of ground in the memorial park.

"Something I haven't seen for months." I turn to Ike. "You still keep track of the calendar?"

"Sure. I mark the days off."

"I gave up doing that…shit, I don't even remember when. So what day is it?"

"It's the third of April. Thursday. Why?"

"Because it's spring, Ike. Those are flowers over there. Can you see them?"

I point.

"Are you sure? They don't look much like flowers."

"Well, they're the best nature appears to able to do under the circumstances. I want some for my apartment."

"You're not serious."

"Fucking watch me, Ike."

I leave them both standing there and march to the nearest park entrance. I cross the threshold no longer concerned about the way the trees and grass look. Flowers. God damn it, I'm going to have flowers. Even if they have browny red petals and weedy looking stalks. I'm having them and that's the end of it.

And you know what else? Maybe me coming back with some live flowers will go some way towards explaining why the three of us are back early and why we look so fucking spooked.

The flowers are in a bed where roses used to grow. I get the creeps walking on the shit-coloured grass to reach them because it feels too resilient beneath my feet. I imagine each blade of grass is squirming under my soles to avoid being crushed under my weight.

At the border of the flowerbed, I pause. Guess I'm having second thoughts about this idea. For a start, I don't have the equipment I need to dig the flowers up and I haven't anything to put them in for the walk home. Not far away is a green trash receptacle. I go over to it and lift out the black trash bag inside. There is no waste inside at all and I can't help but imagine a group of wailing Commuters reaching in and eating handfuls of rotten garbage, tears pouring down their faces all the while. The bag is clean, unused. I remove it.

The rest I'll have to do with my bare hands and, once again, I pause.

All around me the park is silent. I look back to the iron railings and, in a gap between lumpy brown vegetation, Ike and Trixie are watching me. They look tense. I look around me and the whole park is moving in barely perceptible waves. At first, I think it's a breeze giving everything a lazy sway. It's as though we're all under water and a current is making everything undulate so slowly you can't quite see it. Even I'm moving. I look at the flowers. They are moving too, though I have to watch so carefully to see it I still believe I'm imagining it. I stick my index finger in my mouth and hold it up. It stays warm. There is no wind. I listen. There is no sound. The trees do not rustle, their leaves do not sigh.

There is no wind.

I look around again, beginning to feel that sense of too much reality, too much present moment. I can't take it all in. I look at the flowers. They are not moving. I look back at the trees. They are not moving. Nothing in the park moves except me because I am freaked, filled up by what we suddenly know. There is nothing in the park to fear.

I kneel and stick my two hands into the earth beneath some flower stems as though they are two shovels. The soil parts easily, a rich, friable mulch. The clump of brown flowers, my little piece of spring, comes free, black roots and all. I place them on the grass, take a few more double handfuls of earth and dump them in the black plastic bag. Then I lift the flowers in and press them into the protection of the soil. I stand, brush my hands off and carefully lift my flowers. They are coming with me to the Station.

The other Stoppers will be amazed.

There's a tension that builds when you don't go out on the Kill Crew. You can find your place on the wall, say, looking out of a window over the street, and keep your weapon handy. This makes you a guardian of the Station, if any Commuters stray too close to the wall, you can shut them down and you can give covering fire for the crew as they exit and return. But Commuters, most of them at least, don't try to get through the wall any more. Just an occasional lost soul will come here now, like the one that broke its teeth on the padlock, and it's easy to believe that they're just as suicidal as we can be at times.

All we do in the Station is wait and we don't even know what we're waiting for. There's no foreseeable end to the problem unless it's to waste every commuter in the city – hundreds of thousands of people slain, a few a night, for uncountable years. Some of the guys have sat down to do the math. If we whack between twenty and fifty Commuters a night, they say, we'll be running a Kill Crew for the next twenty to thirty years. Course the math doesn't work because we can't say how many of us will be left by then. These are the kinds of things you can't help thinking about.

What we lack here in the Station is freedom. We can get out by day and make trips several miles out on foot. On a bicycle you can go even further. As long as you remember that if you want to come back you mustn't go further than the distance you can travel back before nightfall. It's like wearing an invisible leash. We're all trapped here.

If we want to stay alive.

That gets to being a big if.

Human nature is such that we have an instinct to survive like all the other animals. We resist life being taken away from us. Unlike most animals, however, we can also make the choice to end our lives when we see that there's no point in continuing. Each night you don't crew, you sit, either on top of the rubble or peering out through the grille of a shop door or looking down from a fire escape. You've got your gun in your hand and out there in the green haze of the new night you hear the Kill Crew popping heads. You know that it's never going to end. Not if the other cities out there are in the same condition – and they must be seeing as no one has yet arrived to liberate you. The government, the army, the police force they're ancient history. Shit, you've probably wasted a minor politician or two without even realising. You'll definitely have shot a few desk-jockey cops.

In the daytime, you do your best to clear away the bodies – bodies that never decompose – because you don't want to be tripping over them come sundown on a tough shift. You build walls with bodies but the other Commuters climb them easily. At night you make a mess again. Cleaning crews go out again in the daytime. In between you pass time as though you're in some kind of penal colony. You scratch the days off one by one if you're like Ike. Or, if you're like me, you stopped counting a long time ago.

The tension builds on nights when you don't go out.

On the nights you go out, you blast the tension away.

But you lose sight of a reason for doing it.

You find more reasons for doing it to yourself. So easy. Suck on Kane or Abel. Thumb the death comma. Simple. Or, like the many wistful souls we've lost, you just take a walk as though everything was normal. Just take a walk and don't ever come back to the Station. In that final act they must find some freedom. But only some. None of us curse them. We all understand. The worst thing about it is knowing it could be you next time. Just a little change of attitude is all it takes.

Chapter Seven

Over a camping stove, Ike boils a tin of asparagus soup we found at the deli. We also found some rye crackers and on those we have spread wild boar pâté. We have a big jar of kosher dill pickles and some pimento-stuffed green olives in olive oil. It makes a change from spam and beans.

In the corner, Trixie is playing solitaire, a game I showed her how to play today because I wasn't in the mood to roll dice. Part of me never wants to play another board game – bored game – ever again. Part of me wants a reason never to have to.

Ike opens a bottle of Montepulciano, sniffs the cork and nods in approval. I don't give a shit what it tastes like as long as it takes the edge off my nerves. Right now I am wired tighter than a time bomb.

"Ready for some soup, Trixie?" Ike asks.

"Nuh uh. Just give me the wieners."

We found wieners too. Big ones in brine in a large glass jar. None of us have eaten a fresh vegetable for as long as we can remember. It doesn't make any difference to Trixie. All she wants is processed meat and ketchup. I guess tomatoes are almost vegetables even if they're not fresh. I guess asparagus is too. My stomach growls and I'm reassured that I haven't lost my appetite. Creatures that don't want to eat don't want to live. I'm thankful for my ravening.

On a second camping stove, Ike fries wieners.

"Come and get it," he says.

"I want to eat 'em while I play."

"You come and sit with us. The game'll still be there in five minutes."

There is silence and I fear he's really gone too far this time. Why doesn't he understand that Trixie is fragile, already broken inside somehow? He can't stomp around on her that way.

Trixie stands up from her cards, approaches and then kneels beside Ike. He hands her a plate with two scorched dogs. She takes it. He hands her the ketchup.

"Eat plenty of that red stuff. It's good for you."

She smiles.

"Soon as you finish you can go back to your solitaire, Trixie. I just wanted us to be together while we eat. We've all lost our families but that's no reason to behave like we can't make new ones. We can pretend it's old times until we find some new times."

"I never ate with my…family."

Either of us could say something to her about this but neither of us does.

Ike passes me a glass of wine. He passes one to Trixie. I want to question this but I'll have to do it later, not in front of her. It's not…my place.

He holds up his glass and looks at each of us.

"To finding new times."

We tap our glasses together. Trixie giggles when she drinks her wine and then makes a face.

"Yeugh."

"You'll get used to it," says Ike.

"I don't wanna get used to it."

"Good. More for me."

For a few seconds I almost believe we can pretend to be a family. Then I think very hard about where we are and what we are doing and I know such a thing will never be possible. Not even as a game to pass the time.

I've decided not to tell anyone about the flowers. You never know how they might react.

My apartment is one of the highest in the Station. I've placed the flowers in a blue ceramic pot on the small balcony where people looking up won't see them. Even if anyone looks across from the opposite building they probably won't notice. If they do, I'll say the flowers are silk imitations I found outside. I must be fucking nuts to bring them back in here because whatever is wrong with the Commuters is probably wrong with them too.

But they're only flowers. They can't move or spread. They won't come wailing and forlorn in the night to torment me. If they do, they'll get stomped and burned and that will be the end of them.

They are not beautiful. All they do is remind me that there were once real flowers in the old world. These doppelgangers have petals the brown of a smear of dried blood. Their stalks and leaves are green*ish* but, really, they're brown too. The petals are shaped like daisies but they're much larger. Almost like a kid's idea of what a flower might look like. Except a kid would have ignored the brown crayons.

I've been waiting for a moment alone in which to test their scent. Right now Trixie is out and about somewhere in the Station. She might be with Ike for all I know, developing this thing they have. This entirely unexpected and, I'm quite certain, fragile attempt at a relationship. A father and daughter relationship.

So there's me and there's the flowers. Alone.

I slide open the glass door and kneel down. I bend over the flowers. I allow myself a generous inhalation.

Imagine you're in the countryside somewhere remote, somewhere heather and lichen and moss cover the wet ground. Imagine you've dug a few inches into the earth and forced your face down in there. That filth and readiness, that deep fecundity, that feeling of soil on your lips and nose, it's almost offensive it's so alive. But it does not smell perfumed in the way I'd hoped. It's the opposite of that. These flowers smell of rot and decay just like the mulch of the richest, blackest earth. It's offensive because it smells of potential and of growth. A smell from which all things – any things – may spring.

I can't move fast enough once I realise what's going to happen. My vomit comes in one spasm and I am empty.

I dump the flowers back into the black sack I brought them home in before I even think of clearing up the puke. I know which smells worse. I lay the bag down so that the air can escape and I crush the flowers into their tainted humus beneath the soles of my boots. When the bag is good and compressed, I pick it up and walk down the many flights of stairs to the incinerator in the basement. Next time we light it up, the flowers will be first into the flames.

In my apartment, I swill mouthwash again and again to rid my mouth and nose of the scent of corrupted flowers.

The knock is wrong. I have to think about it for while before I'm able to guess who it is. I put my eye to the peephole just to be sure. I hesitate over whether I'm in or not. He knocks again. I step quietly away from the door to the other side of the room and do my best to sound pissed.

"Get lost."

"We need to talk."

"No we don't."

"All right. I need to talk to you."

"What about?"

"I don't want the whole Station listening."

I move back to the door, snag the security chain and open up. Just three or four inches.

"What?"

"Just let me in, will you?"

"I don't want to talk about Frieda Hartley."

"Neither do I, Sheri. I just want to talk to you. Five minutes."

"Two."

"Okay."

I unlatch the chain and walk away. He enters. Cautiously. Cap in hand, almost, but doesn't say anything. It doesn't suit him, this big man, unable to speak.

"You're down to about ninety seconds."

He looks up, grinding his teeth over whatever he wants to say.

"Shit, Sheri. I need you."

For a moment I misunderstand. Completely. Surely, this isn't how it sounds.

"What are you talking about?"

He sees what I'm thinking and is quick to dispel it.

"On the crew, I mean. Kicking ass. Popping heads. Like you used to."

I look away and shake my head.

"Please, Sheri. It's getting tougher out there."

"I can't do it right now, Monty. If I could, I would – you know me. But I need this time off. I need to get my head together."

"The only way to get your head together is to make Commuters' head bust apart. Get back in the saddle before you lose your courage."

"Don't call me a fucking coward, Spence."

He holds up his hands.

"Jesus, Sheri, I'm not calling you anything."

"You're implying it. You're saying I don't have what it takes to crew any more."

"No. No way. I would never, *could* never say that to you because it isn't true. But I am afraid. I'm afraid for you and I'm afraid for the regulars on the crew. Most of all I'm afraid of what's going to happen to the Station if we don't stay committed to wiping out these freaks of the night."

"You don't need me for that. You've got dozens of regulars that love to pop heads."

Monty sighs. Suddenly he's a smaller man. An older man than I remember from just a few nights ago. There's grey at his temples. Has he had that all this time or has it sprouted there since the last time I saw him? Monty Spence is tired. I can see it now. He's exhausted. When was the last time *he* didn't crew, I wonder? I can't remember. Monty's always been there.

He leans back against the wall for support.

"Whether you know it or not, Sheri, every stopper in this Station sees you as something of a trailblazer. You're one of the few women who chooses to crew. Not only that, you're out there more often than most of the guys. You crew almost as much as I do. That means something to people. It's important. But what it means when you don't crew is even more important. Every stopper's wondering why you're not out there. You know what it does to people's heads when things don't go right in this place. There's a black shadow that stalks every soul in the Station and you know its name. If they think you're giving up, that's another reason not to keep going themselves."

"Fuck you, Monty. You're blaming the future mass suicide of the Nielsen and McKinley Station on me just because I haven't crewed for a few nights."

I'm trying to make a joke of something that can't ever be funny. I'm trying to exaggerate something that cannot be any worse than it already is.

"Yes. I am. You have to keep this Station alive. Whether you like it or not, whether you're scared or not, there's only one way you can do that. Pick up your guns and join the next shift. Get out on the Kill Crew, Sheri. Do it tonight before this whole place melts down."

I feel guilty enough about things without Monty giving me this speech of his. If he knew what was in my mind he'd probably deny me the privilege of suicide by shooting me himself. The fact is, Monty doesn't understand what's really going on. He doesn't have a clue. All I'm trying to do is stay safe, keep out of harm's way a little longer.

Course, now, all that's out of my hands. If I want any kind of future, my schedule for the next few evenings at least is already written in the diary.

I'll be on the Kill Crew.

Chapter Eight

The Commuters are changing. It's taken everyone by surprise. Especially tonight's crew. Why it's taken all this time and why this is happening so suddenly, I can't tell. No one knows why.

Tonight has been too awful for me to take it all in. We took a hammering out there and I don't think it's one we're going to recover from. I don't want to remember it but I'll try because it's important. People should know what happened. You know what I mean, don't you? – if there are still people after we're gone.

It comes back to me in flashes, in bytes, disordered:

We prepare in an alley because we're going over the wall tonight. I feel resolved about crewing again and I know that's down to my history on the job. I've done it ever since I popped my first head from a first floor window. It became a requirement. I've served far more than an apprenticeship out there; I'm inured. And I'm trained. As near to a soldier as a civilian will ever be, acting on reflex and the education provided by exposure to night after night of extremity. I'm an old hand.

And then I snap one of my laces as I tighten my boots and all that confidence bleeds out. I sit for way, way too long studying the frayed end poking from a boot eye and the frayed end in my hand. Paralysed. It's a really bad fucking sign, something like this, a ripple in the placid pond of the way things ought to be. The ripples reach all the way to the shore and I come out of it. But I come out with no strength and no belief.

Sure, you could say the night went bad because I believed it would, that I created my reality out of my state of mind. You could say it was all my fault. To which I say, fuck you. Fuck you because you weren't even there. You haven't had to live through this shit. Harsh, I know. Maybe what you've survived is worse than what we've faced here at the Station. I don't know. I just feel like you don't really understand anything that's happened here. I can say that because, truly, none of us know. Especially not me, the future ghost of Sheri Foley – if ghosts still happen in this new, silent world.

By coincidence, we head out to the memorial park. I think Monty wants to make an easy night of it. Ease me back in gently. My re-laced boot feels wrong around my ankle but there's nothing to be done about it out here. Because of what the three of us saw that day, I'm nervous about being here. There's so much the crew could discover. So much we don't want them to know.

The park is alive. In the greenish phosphorescence of the night, we see it swaying. Once again I feel like we're all underwater. It saps your strength. You doubt your ability to run. The night is a dream, the air is so thick it holds you. When the chase begins, you'll never get away.

And there will be a chase because the park is full of Commuters. Like sea-grass they bend in some invisible current down here at the bottom of the ocean. The seven of us – the sacred, ordained, blessed seven – stop and stare. The Commuters undulate as one and we know they will not come for us yet. Each of us knows from the movement we're seeing that the Commuters are stuck for the moment. They have grown roots deep into the park's soil and perhaps, below its surface they are one. One mind. One body. One intent.

This intelligence of theirs dwarfs us. Everyone feels it. All along we've felt as though the Commuters were stupid, lumbering shells. The remains of the people they once were. Now we know that's not true. They are greater than the sum of their parts and we, by comparison are not. We are the last healthy cells to succumb to a virus, our macrophagic days of head-popping, of commuter stopping, are coming to an end. Our enemy has ceased to be an army of unthinking particles, it has become an organism. A leviathan. We no longer have the equipment with which to fight it off.

Running?

No.

Sprinting.

Backs to them, not even bothering to fire over our shoulders or turn and be more accurate. There isn't time. We're routed, panicking, no formation. This is no dream. What seemed like molasses has become wind on our faces. Our boots batter the streets as we try to escape them. Someone trips, I don't even look to see who it is. I know they won't get up again. The whole city of Commuters, numbering thousands I can't even attempt to count, are coming for us. I do not want to be taken while I still have a chance.

There's a single gunshot behind me followed by the sound of a body hitting the blacktop and the clatter of an orphaned gun. I know what happened without looking.

Five of us keep running.

All I can see is the roots that the Commuters are using as legs now, roots like the legs of spiders, roots like the spindly digits of a too-many-fingered hand. They are very, very fast. They poured through the gates of the memorial park like an insect army. They scaled its iron fences just as easily. Their suits and skirts are torn and filthy and still they weep the pleading tears of the damned.

I drop Kane.

I unstrap Abel and my ammo pack and abandon them in favour of greater speed.

At the Station, the ladders are already over the wall. I'm first to arrive and I hit the ladder hard. Then I'm climbing. Gunfire erupts from every window on this side of the wall. They've all seen. They're all there.

"I need a gun. Give me a fucking gun."

Someone hands me an AK. Not my kind of weapon but there's no time to be picky. I find a free step, aim over the wall and open up. Whatever's inside the Commuters' heads it isn't brains any more. But they still stop when you hit them there. The gunfire is painful, pushes my eardrums in. Gunpowder turns the air bitter. The smoke blurs my vision.

Me and Viktor Lockwood are the only ones to return from tonight's crew. The Commuters have plucked Stoppers out from behind the wall for the first time ever. They used their roots to do it. Dawn is coming. No one speaks yet.

Monty Spence is gone.

I suspect it was he who took matters into his own hands out there tonight, the one who let a gun speak his final word.

We lost thirty Stoppers tonight. The Station's helm is torn away. Rudderless, we arrive drifting on the morning.

For Ike, Trixie and me, a moment has come. Perhaps a moment we should have exploited days ago. I can't help but think we've left it too long. Everything has changed. Maybe the three of us are suicides when you come right down to it.

Perhaps they think it's odd, the other Stoppers. Odd that the three of us are out with our shopping carts again the day after a massacre. We go armed – I insist Ike and Trixie take weapons too because everything is different now. As we push our empty carts away from the walls of the Station I feel like running. It's obvious Ike and Trixie are making a real effort to slow their pace too but they aren't doing a great job. I hope anyone watching will assume we're walking fast because we're terrified.

At the memorial park, apart from the drab colours, nothing has been disturbed. We could have imagined thousands of people dancing beneath the trees, their legs taproots that stretched who knows how far down into that welcoming soil. The thought of it makes me gag. I put a fist to my mouth and swallow back the spasm.

We trundle our carts to the toy store, open the doors and push them inside.

I'm so much happier carrying nothing but guns even if they are unfamiliar. Kane and Abel are no more, taken by the Commuters. I was sure I'd find them outside the walls along with the other dropped or abandoned weapons but they were gone. I'm concerned that the Commuters have taken an interest in firearms. If they ever attacked in that way, the Station would be finished within a day. Half a day.

Or maybe just an hour. Perhaps, in the way the Jews did at the siege of Masada, every remaining stopper would end their own lives. I can't see it ever happening that way though, the Commuters are too interested in taking us alive. They'll do it one by one if they have to; they'd rather do that than kill us off.

Past the deli we find the entrance to the underground car park and walk into the gloom. The hi-lux is parked on the second level down but already we can see the Commuters that line the walls and the floors and ceilings, woven there by their own roots and branches. This was how we saw them that first time, though the growth of plant-like tendrils was less obvious that day. Each commuter had the beginnings of fine filamental rootlets sprouting from the edges of their clothes. We thought it was some kind of hair or pin-mold to begin with. But each time we returned the growth had continued until the resemblance to roots was too obvious to ignore.

We were terrified that first day. We needed to get farther down into the car park but the Commuters' bodies covered every surface. We tested their response with a broom handle first, poking harder and harder until the shaft of wood penetrated a Zegna suit and the tissue beneath without eliciting a response. We kicked them then, half heartedly at first – the way you might nudge a body discovered in the woods. But soon it became kicking and the three of us were booting into the first row of bodies and letting out cries created by months of pent up frustration. Swearing and cursing the Commuters and their miserable, endless onslaught upon the Station. Hating them for wrecking our world and taking all the good things away from us. Particularly satisfying was steel toe-capping a commuter's head until the skull gave way because then you knew they wouldn't stand up again. Ever.

Laughing, crying, exhausted, we jumped into the hi-lux and drove it over the bodies, almost feeling through the tyres the tearing and snapping of flesh and bone beneath us. It was more satisfying than driving over giant bubble wrap. Ike put the headlights on and we descended to the second sublevel. He parked around a corner where even someone looking for the car might not have seen it straight away. The truck had left ruts in the bodies and that was the way we walked back out of there into the light of day.

We've been back many times since, watching the progressive changes in the Commuters and wondering over our timing. The back of the truck is full now, so full that its high suspension has dipped right down to obscure the top of the rear wheels.

What we got:

Water, canned and dried foods, fuel, tents and survival gear, warm clothes for the outdoors, guns and ammo enough to last a year of skirmishing, games, cigarettes. Best of all, we got wheels.

What they got: Uncountable numbers, unpredictable requirements, insomnia.

And in the Station all they got is the suicide blues. We can't stay there any more.

It would be the ultimate fuck-you for Ike to drive within earshot of the Station. Ever since the first day that engine started up, we've been paranoid someone heard it and has been looking for it behind our backs. We were far enough away from the Station that no one did. Maybe we should drive past. If this car works, maybe others do now. Maybe it would give them a reason to go and search for their own vehicles and make a break for the country. Or maybe they'd just come after us for what we've done. I could understand them doing that.

The driving isn't as simple as I thought it would be. Ike has to manoeuvre in and out of plenty of abandoned cars and trucks in many parts of the city. Even on the freeway, there's no easy route through. But I don't care so much about the speed. Even like this we'll be far outside the city come nightfall. Far away from the Commuters and into the country where, I pray, things will be different. Normal again, or as normal as they can be.

"Do you feel sorry?"

Trixie doesn't seem to have addressed the question to anyone in particular. I'm about to answer but Ike doesn't give me the chance.

"Sorry about what?"

"For leaving them all back there?"

"We've already talked about this."

"Yeah, but now we're doing it."

"You know what, Trixie, it comes down to one very simple fact. If we wanted to stay alive, we had to do this."

"Maybe sometimes it's better to make a sacrifice."

We must both hear the note of self-destruction that this idea rings with.

"If there was something worth saving, if there was something it was possible to save, then maybe. But in this case, *we* are what it is worth saving." Ike places his hand on Trixie's bare knee. At the same time, he smiles at me in the rear-view mirror. She looks over at him with a kind of resigned neutrality. His hand squeezes her flesh for several moments, like someone testing the ripeness of fruit, then withdraws. Again the rear-view smile to me.

I stare out the window at what we've been missing all these months.

Chapter Nine

Whatever happened to the city happened to the suburbs. It happened to some of the countryside too.

But when we get forty miles or so beyond the city limits, the foliage and grass ceases to be the brown of stale menses. Gradually, the green of the earth returns like colour to a sickly face. In spite of everything, I begin to relax. Only a little – I'm sitting back here with a fucking shotgun across my lap so I'm not, like, all peace and love or whatever. But some of the tension that has made a lair in my muscles releases. Someone unpicking stitches that hold a wound too tightly closed.

Surely, now, my period will start. Now that we've escaped. But I don't yet believe we have escaped. Which of us can say what will happen after nightfall? Nothing is any more certain than it was before the massacre. All we've done is change location.

Oh yeah, and reduce our numbers. And leave the sanctuary of our walls.

It's so easy to forget what freedom means when you're a prisoner. All you see is the romance of being unfettered the way you think you used to be. But you were guarded in your incarceration, protected by the mundane and the routine. Freedom's twin is uncertainty and she is at our sides now the city lies behind us.

"Ike?"

"What?"

"You still been marking off the days on your calendar?"

"Sure."

"So what day is it today?"

"I guess it's Wednesday the sixth of May."

"May? Are you sure?"

"Yeah, I'm sure. I looked this morning before we left."

Trixie cranes around to take a look at me. Ike's missed the tightness in my throat or maybe I just covered it well. But not well enough to fool Trixie. She doesn't ask me anything. She just looks for a few seconds and then turns away.

In the late afternoon we wind our way up into the hills. The roads are clear now with occasional vehicles abandoned on the soft shoulder – they look like they ran out of gas but who really knows?

The world looks completely normal out here. Except it's real silent and unmoving. I notice this whenever we stop to go to the 'bathroom'. I haven't seen a single bird or animal. There's no wind. No traffic noise. No humming power lines. So it's all wrong, it's more silent than it ought to be. There's certainly been no sign at all of other people. Was that what I'd expected? Or had I hoped to find others out here? People like us, clinging on, waiting for something, letting the animal inside them keep them alive.

I can't say if I'm disappointed or glad. It's not confusion. It's blankness. I'm unable to respond to normality. If this is normal.

Before it gets too dark, Ike pulls over in a broad car park that was once a lookout back over the flat plain and the city far behind us.

"We'll camp here."

"Outdoors?"

Trixie is incredulous. We've explained this but she hasn't taken it in.

"In a tent," I tell her.

"Right. A tent outdoors."

"Yes. A tent outdoors."

"Will we be safe?"

"We'll take turns keeping watch until morning."

"Not me."

"No. Not you," I say.

And I think about that. There's only three of us now. Sooner or later, she'll have to learn. Ike is putting up the tent, a really spacious one that can be moved and re-anchored once it's up. He going to place it in the L-shape made by the hi-lux and a practically vertical rock face where machines cut out the car park.

I pick up my backpack and shotgun.

"Come here, Trix. I've got something I want you to see."

I walk to the railings and look out over the grassy plain. Out there are windmills and farms and power lines and the freeway that turned into the road that brought us here. Hazy in the distance and purpling in the early evening light, the city looks almost normal. Nothing moves but us. The urge is to move very quietly not to go whooping and hollering. I place my pack beside me and show Trixie how I like to hold a shotgun, like a girl who got a giant cock for her birthday.

"A gun like this could be the best friend you ever have. It'll do exactly what you tell it to. And, if you treat it with respect, it will save your life again and again."

"I don't want to do this."

"I know you don't. But if you want to stay alive, you've got to grow up. Real fast."

Knowing there's nowhere else to go and knowing darn well I'm right in what I'm telling her, Trixie watches as I show her what's what. As the minutes go by, she forgets her reluctance. It becomes inquisitiveness. Once or twice she giggles. From the back door of the hi-lux I see Ike watching and smoking quietly.

The first time she fires the shotgun I can see her eyes glisten with shock and realisation. Trixie has discovered power. There's no point in me hoping she'll use it wisely. Out here we're way beyond the importance of wisdom. We are ruled by the whiteness of survival and the blackness of suicide. In such a world, guns become our lovers. Trixie's got a big crush.

Once I'm happy she's safe to fire the shotgun, I take an empty soda can from the garbage bucket people would have used when stopping here to take in the view. I set it up on one of the posts of the safety railing. I take her back ten feet but she wants to go back twenty. I shrug. From the hip, she fires and the soda can disappears in a ripple of torn aluminium. I set up eight more cans. Trixie reloads and pumps. Shot after shot cracks off the hillside behind us and booms out across the plain. She hits five out of eight. Not bad. Certainly good enough to pop heads at close range if the need arises.

By the truck, Ike crushes out his butt and resumes unloading.

Through the night Ike and I sleep two hours and watch two hours until dawn.

I'm the one out there when the light rises. It takes a long time to happen.

There's been no moon and no stars – cloudy and disappointing. It meant neither of us could see our hands in front of our faces. Sitting on a fold-out camping chair with a brand new shotgun – I haven't even named him yet – it's so dark you keep watch with your ears. You turn your head like a radar dish trying to catch sounds before anything can come too close. But there's no sound. Soon you are nothing but your own thoughts in the blackness unsure even if you are awake or dreaming. The first thing dawn does is fill your vision with the spirits of shapes so faint you don't believe they're real. You don't understand what you're seeing.

Over an hour or more the ghosts become familiar things. Rocks and trees, the tent and truck. They come to life slowly and you realise the value of time. Even as slowly as this, nothing stays the same. You realise you ought never to sleep. Every moment should be observed in its precious unrepeatability. By the time the sun rises I'm glad to be alive. I don't remember the last time I could honestly say that to anyone.

Regardless of everything, I have hope. It lives inside me.

In the tent, warm in his sleeping bag, the slender man thinks about the girl.

She is not far away from him. He can hear her breathing in the darkness. He shares her exhalations. For now that's as much of her as he can possess but it's enough. He asks himself can he really be considering the same things he's always considered. Everything in the world has changed but he has not. He seems not to have responded. He wonders if that's why he's survived this long. Maybe it's because he has not accepted the new world.

He is honest with himself. There is no denying his true feelings. He could lock them down, use his will against himself, true. But why? Why in this new time when there is no longer any certainty that such self control matters. Restrain himself for what reason? For what future? He suspects the world has ended, that until his own death comes there is nothing for him but the tiny anarchy of doing whatever he wishes.

And yet he has not. Something in him, some conditioning or aspect of decorum fights the chaos of his simpler desires. It's not religion. It's the understanding that while there are still three people on earth, while there are still two people, there is society and society has value above his wants. He could be out here alone, supplied well enough to last out his life driving from town to town but how long before the solitude killed him?

The man knows the truth about himself and does not deny it. Truth lives within him but it remains unshared. Does that make him a liar? Deceitful? Is untruth as alive in him as it is in the others? Should he even care so much about what people call truth? Who is he to even contemplate its importance? In the old world they would have called him a bad man, if they'd caught him, they'd have removed him from society. Now he is part of all that's left of society. Perhaps in this new world, things could be different.

No. Of course they could not. He is a vehicle for the lies of the old world and he knows it very well. Everything has changed but nothing really changes. What was bad before is still bad now and that is still not enough to prevent it.

All this he thinks as he shares space and night with the girl, as he breathes her breath and smells her exudations. Nothing he thinks changes the way he feels or what he knows he will one day allow himself to do. He wonders why this is his only constant; the worst part of himself.

We eat Bush's beans and drink black coffee for breakfast but I don't have much appetite.

Trixie and I help to pack up the tent, learning a little about how it works as we go. Then we're driving again. As we rise higher into the hills, my ears pop. The road gets twistier and Trixie gets car sick. We stop for her to puke but she's just going to have to get used to it. About a second after I think this, I begin to feel nauseous myself. Pretty soon Ike has to pull over for me and suddenly I'm not so pragmatic about how we should cope with sickness. Having seen both of us heave up, I wonder if Ike is going to come out in sympathy but he doesn't. He just drives. He's quiet today.

We've filled the truck with gas a couple of times from our jerry cans but Ike is concerned that we need more. The next fuel Station we find, he hauls a manhole cover up in the forecourt and uses a rope and bucket to dip for fuel. There's hundreds of thousands of gallons down there, he tells us. Enough to drive us back and forth across the country indefinitely.

That evening we're much higher up. It's not hills any more, it's mountains. None of us smells too great in the confines of the truck and there's a lingering air of vomit.

"Let's find somewhere near water, Ike. We could all do with a freshen up."

"Sure. Want to stop soon? We've probably gone far enough for today."

Trixie nods eagerly. These roads haven't been kind to her.

Around a few more bends, like an answer to a prayer, we find a stream flowing fast. Not much farther on, there's an escape lane for trucks with brake problems and that's where Ike parks up.

"Why don't you make camp while Trixie and I go and get washed up?"

"At your service," says Ike. "Want me to make dinner too?"

"I'll do that when we come back. You can have your wash while I prepare it."

Trixie and I walk back up the hard shoulder and off the road to the stream. I walk a little ways along it to be sure we're far from the road even though I'm pretty sure there'll be no one passing by. I strip down naked and dip a face cloth into the water.

"Brrr."

Goose bumps spread top to toe in a single wave before the water even touches my skin. I take some soap and lather up. Trixie looks embarrassed.

"Come on, Trix. Might as well get used to this. No telling how long we'll be on the road for. We're both women so there's nothing to be worried about." Trixie starts to undress and the moment she's naked I feel certain that Ike is watching. I turn to look up the rise. He should be on the other side of it setting up our camp site. I don't see him so maybe he is. Trixie seems more worried about me seeing her though. She rinses her arms and feet but that's all. I won't stand for it

"Come on, get yourself clean. Everything, Trixie. It's important."

"You're not my mother."

"No. None of us have mothers any more. Do as I tell you and make it quick."

The zero tolerance approach seems to work and soon she's soaping everything up.

"That's the idea."

I'm freezing so I make the wash quick. When I sit down on a rock to wash between my toes I get a shock. There's something growing off my feet. I stop. My heart misfires once. Twice. I don't want this to be what I think it looks like. I cross one leg over the other to take a closer look. There are white hair-like tendrils growing from the soles of my feet. I take hold of one and pull. It doesn't feel like a hair. It feels like it's part of my skin. I'm nauseous again in the space of a second. Fuck it. Fuck this. I yank the tendril and it breaks off. I breathe in sharply. Pulling hairs out shouldn't hurt that way. Hairs shouldn't be growing on the soles of anyone's feet. And they shouldn't leak sap when you pull them.

No. Not this. Not now of all times. I'm pretty sure I've got Ike's child growing inside me. Much as I hate the idea I know that if I take the child to term and it survives that it will be a child for the new world, a tiny fragment of hope for the future. But now, after only a few days of suspecting I might be pregnant for the first time in my life, I see that I'm pregnant two ways. The new world is in me. Somehow it got inside.

Then I remember the flowers. And I start to cry.

Chapter Ten

Trixie is so self-conscious about her ablutions that I manage to dry myself and hide my feet inside my boots. The tears I can't hide so easily.

"What's wrong?" She asks.

I pull in a breath that goes right to the pit of my guts and let it go. My strength goes with it.

"Everything. Nothing. I don't know."

She reaches out. Touches my forearm. It's a very adult gesture; almost motherly. It takes me by surprise. Her eyes are full of knowledge.

"I know how fucked up all this is. Most of the time I can't fit the fuckedness of it in my head but sometimes I get a flash of what's happened to us. A flash of it is all my mind can take, I think. All this time I've been so drowned by my old shit I haven't really noticed the new shit we're in. It's like I've been playing one bad song off a CD over and over. My song of shit. But getting away from the Station, seeing the world outside and how quiet it is…It's made me feel different. Like I've been acting spoiled this whole time. Now I can see the trouble we're in better, I know my own troubles don't mean anything. I might as well forget them. I should be thinking about the future, right Sheri? Just leaving the bad stuff behind."

My tears get worse. I can't control them. Jesus Christ, if you're still up there, she's only a kid and listen to her. She's had to grow up overnight. What the hell is wrong with this world? I take a hold of Trixie – never mind what she's lived through before I met her, we need this contact – and I squeeze her to me and weep into her greasy, dirty hair.

"Promise me, Trixie…" I have to speak between my own sobs. "Promise me whatever happens you won't let him come near you. Never let anyone hurt you again."

God, I don't want to let go of this girl. I don't want to let go of this life. Look how we've fought. Look what we've survived to make it this far. We were so nearly free and now I'm fucked. I hold her so tight it hurts my arms but she doesn't try to get away from me. I don't know how long we stand that way. Letting go of her brings fresh tears.

"You don't have to worry about me, Sheri. I've changed. No one's going to use me any more. Anyways, I've got a new friend now."

I hadn't noticed it but she's packing. From her slim, bike-courier's backpack she draws out a customised shotgun with a snub barrel. She grins.

"Meet Barnaby."

I giggle through the tears. I can see there's significance to the name but I stop myself from asking. She sees this.

"It was my brother's name."

I nod. That's all.

"Is it loaded?"

"Eight shells."

"Good. Keep it that way."

We start back towards the escape lane campsite.

"Trixie?"

"What?"

"I…it doesn't matter."

"What, Sheri?"

"Never mind. I was going to say something dumb. For once I stopped myself."

She holds my hand.

How do you tell your only friend in the world you're not who they think you are? How do you say goodbye?

Ike comes out for his watch.

"Go back to sleep."

"It's my turn."

"I don't care. I'll wake you when I get tired. I want to stay out here a while longer."

"Is everything okay?"

"It's fine."

Ike stretches his spine out.

"Can I sit with you for a while?"

"It's a free country."

"I'm not sure that's true."

"You know what I mean."

He sits in the camp chair beside me and lights up a cigarette. I hesitate and then reach out for one.

"You sure?"

"What the fuck do I have to lose now? I should have taken it up months ago."

I put the cigarette between my lips. It feels a lot fatter than it looks. Ike cups the flame from his lighter and I lean in to draw on the cigarette. I've seen it done so many times by so many people, especially by him. I pull the smoke in, it bites, I get a head rush and breathe out. My heart hammers and I feel sick. I don't care. I take another drag. Pretty soon the feelings even out and I'm smoking like I've done it all my life.

Finally, Ike says:

"I've missed…being with you."

"Bullshit."

"Sheri, what do y–"

"I know what kind of man you are, Isaac."

He's quiet for a moment, then, in a very low tone:

"What does that mean?"

"It means I know you've used me to get close to Trixie. It means I know why you would do something like that. Let one more lie come my way and see what happens."

He's quiet. I know he wishes I'd kept my voice down but there's no way he can say that. Is he thinking about his options? Coming up with a new angle? I don't care. I don't give him the chance to spin me any more yarns.

"Our relationship has become one of necessity. We watch each other's backs. We work together until we find something or someone out here who can help us. When that time comes, I'm taking Trixie away from you. Far away. And if you try to push this thing with her, I'll kill you myself, Ike. I fucking swear to God."

He's silent. He drops his butt to the dirt but doesn't bother to stomp it out. Before he gets to the tent, I say:

"Leave me your smokes and lighter."

He hesitates and then comes back to hand them to me.

"Sleep well, Ike. I'll be watching over you."

I've lived in the city all my life so I don't know anything about the stars. Even when the power went off the city glowed at night time. Sure, I've seen a star or two on a clear night but nothing like this.

Above me the blackness shimmers. It's almost liquid. Someone scattered diamonds over a pool of tar and now that pool ripples. Except it isn't like that at all. It's infinitely more beautiful than any attempt of mine to describe it to you. I don't know whether to be terrified or reassured by the size of space, whether to have faith in the order of things or be convinced of the randomness of it all. I see my tininess in the scheme – or chaos – of things, even the tininess of our whole planet. The world is an insignificant dot and I am lost upon it. The stars will be up there after I am gone and after Earth is gone. Shimmering. Reflecting the thoughts of…well, someone, I hope. People, I hope.

And then I wonder, do the Commuters look up? Do they know about stars? Do they care? Is that where they came from or did we create them ourselves somehow? Before I brought those flowers back to the Station, I'd never have had the opportunity to know the answer to those questions. Now there's a possibility I will find out. I'm not sure I want that.

What's the point of me? What's the point of my baby? Is it infected like me or is it still a pure person? Does it really matter either way?

Well, it may not matter to the stars but it matters to me.

Theses are my options:

Leave Ike and Trixie to go on without me and wait it out. She'll be safe now, I feel her strength of purpose. She's become a woman long before her time. I could stay here in the mountains until I give birth. If the baby comes out human I could try to look after it but by then maybe the Commuters roots will be in my brain as well as my feet. Maybe I'd just turn it into another commuter the moment it popped out. If it came out commuter and I was still human enough, would I kill it? Could I? I realise I can't leave Ike and Trixie until I know what's happening to me for sure. I need them.

Or I could walk out into the darkness now, somewhere down by the stream, and blow my fucking brains out while they're still human enough to let me pull the trigger. The old stopper values coming through, the will to suicide as fresh as ever. But I don't have the luxury of calling myself a stopper any more, do I? I don't know what I am.

I could tell the others and see what ideas they have. I know what Ike's would be.

Or I could tell Trixie. Let her keep watch over me. Let her decide when I've become a danger to them both. Let her be the one to decide what to do with my child. If that doesn't affirm her adulthood, nothing will.

The trick with information is how much to give and to whom.

I think I have an idea.

Chapter Eleven

No wonder I'm exhausted when morning comes. I haven't slept all night.

The three of us eat breakfast in silence. I'm the only one who can't raise much of an appetite. I spoon the tinned beans and mushrooms around my plate trying to find something that looks good to eat. None of it does. In the end I hand my portion to Trixie. Ike barely looks up from his plastic plate.

Instead of food, I pull out the nearly empty pack of smokes, shake one out and light it. Trixie's eyes widen but whatever look is on my face is enough to stop her from opening her mouth. I suddenly wonder what it's like to roll your own cigarettes with your favourite tobacco instead of smoking something that was churned out of some huge fucking factory. I'll probably never know the answer to that one.

I blow out the words –

"I'm pregnant."

– on a stream of smoke. The smoke muffles the sound of my voice but both of them look up.

Ike stops chewing and swallows.

"What did you say?"

"I'm going to have a baby. Your baby, Ike."

Trixie's eyes open wider. Ike is motionless. Trixie puts down her plate – my plate.

"All *right*," she says. "Oh my god. I can't believe it. That is *awesome*."

Ike, on the other hand, appears to have lost the faculty of speech. I hand him a cigarette, lean over and light it for him. He draws. Looks from my face to Trixie's and back again. Then he looks down. At my belly.

"Are you serious, Sheri?"

"I'm dead fucking serious, Ike."

"But you told me you had your–"

"I lied."

He doesn't look pleased.

"How do I know you're not lying to us right now?"

"You don't, Ike. But time will prove I'm telling the truth."

"You probably shouldn't be smoking, you know. It's bad for the–"

"Shut up, Ike. Just shut up right now and don't ever start thinking you can tell me how to live. Your position is one of responsibility. That's all. You protect me – us – and you make sure we come first in every decision. This is my baby, Ike. Mine."

"But Christ, Sheri, I'm the goddamned fath…"

His eyes sharpen. He gives a resigned, humourless snort.

"I don't know you at all, do I?"

I say nothing.

Ike rises and walks away to where he can smoke with his back to us. Smoke and think. Assuming he's capable of such higher functions.

"Why are you so mean to him?"

"Because he's scum, Trixie. It's the end of the fucking world and that's the man we've got to take care of us. Anyway, what do you care? You know what he wants. How can you protect him?"

"I'm not protecting him. I know he's screwed up. But that doesn't mean the three of us shouldn't get along. Otherwise every day is going to be hell. I'm done with that shit, Sheri. Let's try and be nice to each other."

"Be nice until when? When you find him pinning you down in the middle of the night? When I'm gone I won't be able to protect you any more. I won't be able to watch your back. This isn't about being nice any more, Trixie. It's about staying alive and staying human."

Trixie is pale.

"What do you mean?"

"What?"

"You said 'when I'm gone'. What does that mean?"

I look over to Ike. I think he's far enough away. Maybe he could hear the first part – I don't care if he knows what I think – but he mustn't hear this. I reach over and take her hand.

I tell her what's happened to me. I tell her what I think will happen. I tell her what I think that means.

Suddenly she's not a young woman any more. She's the quiet, broken little girl that I met when we formed the Station all those months ago. She's the silent girl that clung to me like a monkey baby all through the night.

And I'm sorry about that. Truly sorry. But we're way beyond saving each other's feelings now. We're in new territory again. And I don't like it. I don't like it at all.

Ike drives us through the mountains but I don't know much about it. I sleep right through the day of switchback bends and the views of snow-topped peaks. Even when they take rest stops, I sleep on.

At dusk, I wake. In time to see we've cleared the mountains. In the distance there's another city. Larger by far than the one we left behind us. Probably one of the largest cities in the world. In this light and at this distance there's no way to tell what has happened there. We've seen no people on the journey. No animals. It can't bode well. But maybe in that city, that huge city, there will be more like us. Greater numbers than we had back at the Station. And maybe they're making a difference. Fighting back better than we ever could.

Ike pulls up in a tree-lined road. From here we can't see much of anything in front or behind. The shelter is pleasant but, of course, it could be dangerous too. He sets up the tent and I make the dinner – instant mashed potatoes and two cans of stew. It actually smells pretty good but even so I can only manage about half of it. This time I split what's left between Ike and Trixie. Just to be fair. Just to be *nice*.

"How're you feeling, Sheri?"

Ike is all concern now. Determined to prove himself a better man. Or maybe he really does care. I don't. I stand up and wander away from the campsite, out beyond the trees further from the road. I can sense the looks passing between Trixie and Ike. I guess they must both be worried and that's good. That's what I wanted. Each of them worried in their own special way. Each of them ready to help me when I need help.

Out here beyond the trees the stars are out again. I want to reach up and pluck them. Pop them into my mouth and swallow suns. I'm excited about going to the new city. I think of all the things there that we can have. Abandoned shops full of everything we could possible ever need. Houses of luxury and beauty – no servants of course but that would be a small matter. Anything we want. It's all there in that city.

And the stars. And the worlds that circle them. We could have all that too if we wanted. Why not? I've got this hunger. Not for food but for satisfaction, for fullness, for a surfeit of everything. I simply want. And isn't that a good thing? Isn't that so much better than the blankness I've been feeling these last months? Isn't it better than the wondering how I'll face the next day, the next night?

I giggle and stifle it. Laughter is too loud in darkness.

I'm alive and full of desire. This is good. I'm changing. Waking up. Me and my baby, we'll go to the city and we'll have whatever we want. And there will be people there to share it with. Yes, we need more people with us.

But then what? After we have everything we could ever want or need; what then? What comes after that?

Something's wrong with my feet. They're pressing against the insides of my boots like they're swollen. And it's–

Ahh. That's better. My roots have split out of the leather and the relief is…god, that feels good. I'm gripping the ground with two hundred fingers. Pulling at it. Taking away from it. In the starlight my hands have become very much like my feet. Long tendrils reach out and wave in the night air. They want to go to the city and take…

…everything.

But what comes after everything? The question just won't go away.

I know what the answer is but I don't want to think about it.

When everything you have is not enough, there is nothing else. You can never be content. An emotion swells within me, coming up fast and huge and I'm not sure I have the strength to hold this kind of feeling. Nothing will ever be enough. Nothing will ever satisfy. And yet, I must pursue satiety. I must consume. I have to at least try to fill the emptiness. The emotion bursts up and out through me, destroying all hope and with it come the bitterest tears.

Beneath the richness of the stars, I howl with loss for what I'll never have.

Sheri was smart. She knew Ike would try to protect her if it turned out she beat the thing that was taking her over. She knew if she made it to term, we'd both look after the baby. But she also knew both us wouldn't hesitate to blow her away if she turned. She had it all worked out.

But she was wrong.

When we heard the wailing we both grabbed our guns and ran out to the field she was standing in. Her hands and feet had roots like claws and she was weeping to the sky. It was awful to hear that sound out here in the country. I'd prayed we'd never hear that sound again. But we'd brought the sickness of the Commuters with us. Inside Sheri.

Inside my best friend and the only woman that ever earned the name 'mother'.

She came towards us, reaching out those arms like all she wanted was to take us both to whatever hell she'd discovered. Ike couldn't raise his shotgun at first. Not until she got real close. I could see the tears in his eyes. He wanted forgiveness and – what do they call it? – redemption, I think. Like the priests give out at confession on Sundays. I couldn't give it to him. Sheri was his last chance at it. His last chance to be a good man. Because of that, he didn't raise his gun until the last possible moment. When he did, he couldn't fire it.

So I stepped up to the plate and I shot my mom. The first person I ever killed and she was the one that mattered most. If the commuter sickness didn't take away her soul, I pray she's in heaven thanking me for it. I know I was only doing what she expected me to do. Just the way she planned it before she lost control.

So, it's just me and Ike now. A man that will never be my father even though he could be my real dad's double, loves me in the same screwed up kind of way.

When we see the brown areas that have spread out from the city, we turn back. There's no reason to get into trouble. We could go in for a few hours while its light but we know what we'll see so what's the point?

Ike finds a road that leads north. He says we're going to Canada. Maybe what happened here didn't happen up there, he says. I don't think he really believes it though. And neither do I.

All we need is a reason to survive. Some sign that there's going to be something else apart from the commuter destruction and the way it's spread through everything. I don't know if we'll find that here or in Canada. I don't know if we'll ever find it anywhere.

I can relax though. Sheri gave me something I can't thank her for even though I want to and I do in my prayers. She taught me how to use Barnaby. I can use him to protect myself from Ike if he stops being a partner and starts trying to be my dad. But the real power she gave me is the power to not be like the Commuters. Not ever. Because if it comes to that, she's given me the power to make my own decision.

She knew that's what she was doing the day she taught me how to shoot. It can't have been easy for her, giving me that power. That means a lot. She gave me the freedom to choose my own way. I think that means Sheri was the only person that ever truly loved me.

Epilogue

We've been driving for two more days since I killed my mom.

More and more, we see the rusty brown fingers of the commuter sickness spreading out into the land, sucking the life out of it. Ike has stopped talking to me now. I guess any moment he might pull the truck over and try to get what he wants from me just once before he gives in to the truth. Fact is, we're running out of places to go.

I slip my hand inside my backpack and finger Barnaby's safety to 'off'.

Lightning Source UK Ltd.
Milton Keynes UK
29 December 2009

147975UK00001B/96/P